Hers to Redeem
The Reclusive Man

Robbie's Roaming

J. L. Dawson

Hers to Redeem
The Reclusive Man

Robbie's Roaming

By J L Dawson

Butterfly Books
PUBLISHING

Cover design by: Virginia McKevitt
Edited by: Amber Smith

ISBN (Paperback) 978-1-7385962-8-7
ISBN (E-book) 978-1-7385962-9-4

A CiP catalogue record for this title is available from the National Library of New Zealand.

First edition, 2023 Butterfly Books Publishing

Contact the author or subscribe to newsletter:
jldawsonauthor@yahoo.com
www.jodawsonauthor.com

Contents

One

"Blast these boots." Robbie grimaced as he stumbled and tripped for the umpteenth time, over the sole, which flapped open at the front. He scowled, stopped by the side of the road, and squatted down. His loyal dog, Ozzie, sat on his hind legs and let his pink tongue dangle to the side as he took a moment to rest.

Robbie lifted his knapsack off his shoulder and dumped it on the ground in front of him. Rustling through the bag, he pulled out a ball of twine. Fishing in his pocket, he grabbed his small knife, sliced a length off the twine, wrapped it around the toe of his boot four times, then tied it in a bow at the top.

He shrugged, thrust the knapsack back over his shoulder, and ruffled the head of his dog. "It's not a very good fix, but it'll get us to the next town, and then hopefully, we can find work and put some food in our bellies." The dog whimpered and rewarded Robbie with a lick to his face. The man stood up abruptly and rubbed his sleeve across his mouth. "Thanks for that, Boy."

He resumed walking, and Ozzie fell into step with him as always. Close to a mile further down the track, he stopped to listen. Ozzie pricked his ears up and stood to attention. Turning back the way he'd come, Robbie noticed two covered wagons approaching. He shrugged, and continued walking.

The front wagon drew up alongside Robbie. "Howdy." A man tipped his hat. A woman sat next to him, and two children poked their heads out from under the canvas.

Robbie nodded to the man but carried on walking.

"Where are you headed?" the man persisted.

"Next town." Robbie shrugged.

"Dusty Ridge?"

"Yeah, I guess."

"Hey, that's where we're headed; got us a ranch just out of town."

Robbie nodded and thrust his hands in his pockets.

"You want to ride with us, Son?"

"Nah, we don't mind walking." He gestured to the dog.

"Okay, please yourself." The man nodded, clucked his tongue to the horses, and continued. The man and woman in the second wagon nodded their greeting as they rumbled past.

Robbie shook his head. "Why'd I turn them down? I've had enough of walking. Don't wanna be beholden to anyone, though. Can't afford to pay 'em." He grimaced. "Gotta find some work. Maybe this town will finally be where we stop roaming, Boy."

Ozzie whimpered.

"Yeah, I know. I say that every town we approach. But surely one day we gotta stop and settle down?" Robbie sighed, ran his fingers through his hair, then thrust both hands in his pockets. He toyed with the knife in his right pocket and old pocket watch in his left as he continued down the road.

Around midday, Robbie came across the two families again. This time parked up and seated on the ground, enjoying their lunch. "Hi there." The man from the first wagon waved to Robbie. "Care to join us?"

Robbie shrugged and kept walking.

"You'd be most welcome, Lad," the second man called. "Plenty to eat."

The smell of their food simmering over the fire was tantalizing. His growling stomach overruled his 'no charity' principle, and he headed in their direction. The first man gestured to a spot opposite him and Robbie sat down with Ozzie next to him.

"Hi, Mister." A boy greeted him; he looked to be about eight years old. He reached a hand out to stroke Ozzie, who nuzzled against his hand.

Robbie nodded to the boy.

A woman sat forward, reached for a bowl, and ladled in some stew. She passed it to Robbie and he mumbled a thank you.

Both couples chuckled as they watched Robbie eat. The first bite told him just how hungry he was. The rabbit stew was delicious, and he soon cleaned his bowl.

"Ya want some for ya dog?" the woman offered. Robbie nodded and passed her his empty bowl, she slopped in a ladle full, and the dog made short work of it.

Having finished his meal, Robbie turned grateful eyes on the people. "Thank you." He remembered the manners Mrs. Bonnie and the pastor had tried to force into him as a child in the orphanage.

"You're most welcome, Lad. When was the last time you ate?" The first man eyed Robbie.

"Two days ago, I think." Robbie shrugged.

"Oh, no wonder you're so hungry."

"What's ya name?" a boy asked.

The man chuckled. "You're right, Son. We better make introductions. I'm Carl Baker; this here's my wife Eva, and our two rascals, Peter and Freddy." He smiled and ruffled the hair of two dark-haired boys. "And we got one on the way." He grinned, and winked at his wife.

Robbie turned his eyes to the other couple. Carl continued the introductions. "This here is my brother-in-law, Eva's brother, Samuel Turner, his wife Edith, and their three children, Matty, Louise, and the little one is Emily."

Robbie nodded. "Robbie."

Carl raised his brows. "Just Robbie or you got a last name?"

"Go by Hall."

The two men looked at each other, squinted, and turned their eyes on Robbie. "What do you mean go by? Isn't that ya name?" Samuel stroked his short beard.

Robbie shrugged and shook his head. "I don't know what my last name is."

The four adults put down their coffee cups and frowned at him. "Do you mind me asking your story?

I never met a man who didn't know his own name?" Carl enquired.

Robbie shrugged. He reached into his top pocket and pulled out a tatty New Testament, opened it, and slipped out an equally tatty photograph. "I go by Hall because that was the name the doctor found here in this little Bible that was my Mama's. It seems it was given by her pa, so I imagine that's her name before she was married. Dunno what her married name was." He shrugged again and passed the small Bible and photograph across to the man. He perused it, showed it to his wife and then brother and sister-in-law, and they passed it back to Robbie, turning their eyes on him in anticipation.

Ozzie put his head in Robbie's lap, and he stroked the dog while he spoke.

"My earliest memory is climbing down off a wagon with the seven other children from an orphanage in the east. The pastor and his wife that looked after us, came West to escape the war for our sake. When I was old enough to ask about who I was, Pastor Wright gave me these." He nodded to the photo and Bible and pulled out the pocket watch to show them. He didn't mention the two rings and cameo he had in his knapsack. "These were all my mother had on her when she was brought to an army hospital in Virginia during the war. They only knew her name was Pearl, and her sergeant husband had been killed at Manassas. From what I understand, it put her into shock and early labor. A soldier from a nearby encampment had brought her to the hospital but had to leave to get back to the regiment; said he'd be back for her when they sent word.

"She told the doctor her first name and little else; she was in a lot of pain and hemorrhaged badly. She struggled to breathe, and by the time I was born, she was very weak. She managed to whisper. 'Robbie for my pa.' Then she passed. The doctor searched her things and found the name Hall. By the time they'd sent word to the encampment, the regiment had packed up and left in a hurry, so no one knew who I was.

"The doctor listed me as 'Robbie Hall' and the hospital gave me to the Hope of Jesus Orphanage, and Pastor and Mrs. Wright raised me. When it became too dangerous for them to stay in Virginia, they raised money to move us all west. That's how I ended up in Colorado. Left them when I was twelve, been roaming ever since."

All eyes were glued to Robbie as he told his story. "All on your own?" Carl asked.

Robbie sighed. He didn't usually tell this much about himself. In fact, he hardly talked this much at all, but these people seemed interested, and he felt oddly at ease with them. "I left with my friend Tim, he grew up with me at the orphanage, but he stayed in Colorado Springs, got a job in the mill, and married a pretty girl. That was about two years ago. Then Ozzie and me, we continued south."

"What do you do to survive?" Eva asked.

Robbie shrugged. "Odd jobs, whatever I can. I been to pretty much every town between here and Colorado Springs, looking for work."

"How come you never settled down?" Edith asked, refilling her husband's coffee cup, and passing a cup to Robbie.

Robbie nodded his thanks, and reached for the cup, took a long slurp, and looked back at them. "Just never found my place, I guess. I'm sure God will show me where it is eventually."

The four adults' faces lit up. "You a Christian, Robbie?" Carl nodded his thanks as Edith passed him a cup.

Robbie shrugged. "I believe in God, the pastor taught us about the Bible and God, and I pray some. Not sure I know much 'bout it all, but I know God is there. I reckon He's looked out for me all these years."

"He has." Eva smiled. "He looks after all His sheep."

Samuel gestured to the tatty New Testament. "You'll find what you need to know in there."

Robbie merely nodded and thrust it back into his breast pocket.

"Well, we better get going; wanna reach Dusty Ridge by nightfall. You wanna ride with us, Robbie? We'd be happy to have you join us," Carl offered.

Robbie looked around nervously.

"Doesn't look like your boots will make it there if ya walk." Sam gestured to the makeshift fix.

Robbie nodded. "If ya wouldn't mind."

All faces lit up. "It'd be our pleasure, Robbie." Carl stood up.

"You can ride with us and we can play with Ozzie." Freddy put a hand out to the dog.

Ozzie nuzzled into his hand and licked Freddy's arm. Freddy giggled and wiped his hand on his shorts.

Robbie did what he could to help them tidy the campsite, carefully extinguishing the fire and heaping dirt on top, just to be cautious.

"We made good time." Carl squeezed Eva's hand as they rolled up to the general store in Dusty Ridge.

Robbie leaped down from the back of the wagon, and Ozzie jumped out next to him. He walked around to the front just as Carl was helping Eva down.

"I'm much obliged for the ride." Robbie began to walk away.

"Robbie, where are ya gonna stay?"

Robbie shrugged. "A barn, maybe the livery if they'll let me; if not, under the stars is fine. Done it before. Gotta find work tomorrow. Ozzie and me gotta eat."

Carl looked at Samuel, who walked up beside him. "We've purchased the Circle A ranch, about a mile yonder. Already got two houses on it. We'll be needing some ranch hands, and I plan to start working with horses. You any good in the saddle?"

"Done some ranch work with my pal Timothy in Colorado Springs."

"You fancy doing some now?" Samuel asked.

"You don't even know me. Why would you take that chance?" Robbie frowned.

"You seem like a decent chap, had a hard go of it. We're willing to give you a chance. There's a bunkhouse out there for the cattle hands. You'd be welcome. Start out riding the range, and we'll see where that leads ya.

"When we came to scout the place in the spring, we met the foreman, Edwards. We've kept him on, and he's been running the place for us till we could come back with our families. He said he'd be needing three or four more men. The previous man's three sons worked for him and went with him when he left." Carl nodded to Robbie.

"What say you?" Samuel asked.

Robbie shrugged and tried hard not to grin. "Yeah, reckon I could."

Carl slapped him on the back. "That's good news, Praise God. We knew He'd bring us the men we need."

"Much obliged."

"Well, we gotta get a few things from the store, but if you don't mind waiting with the children, we'll get you out to the ranch in a jiffy." Carl nodded to him and led his wife into the store.

Robbie nodded and knelt to pet his dog. "Looks like we might have found ourselves a home for a time, Boy. Maybe this will finally be where we belong. Been roaming for far too long." He sighed and leaned against the wagon to wait.

He looked around at the small town. Several small stores and homes lined the dusty street. "Dusty Ridge." He chuckled internally. "Aptly named." He noticed the entire town seemed to be coated in a layer of dust.

*   *   *   *

"Edwards." Carl jumped down from the wagon and shook the foreman's hand.

"Good to have you here, Baker." Edwards raised his hand to shake and nodded up to Mrs. Baker.

Carl gripped his shoulder. "The spread's looking good. Thanks for taking over while we were gone."

"It's fine, Sir. It's what I do." The weathered cowboy nodded.

Robbie walked up alongside them, Ozzie at his heels. Carl nodded and turned to Edwards. "Brought you a new man."

Edwards squinted and eyed Robbie up and down. "You got any experience?"

Robbie shrugged. "Some."

"I'll train ya. Do ya ride, at least?"

"Of course."

"You got a horse?"

"Nah, this is all I got." He gestured to the dog and lifted his small knapsack.

Edwards nodded and grimaced. "Gonna need to get some better gear, boots, and chaps."

Robbie shrugged. "Ain't got no money."

"Don't worry, we'll see to it you have the things you need." Samuel approached.

"Don't want charity; I'm happy to work for 'em."

"Don't worry, we'll work ya hard." Edwards chuckled. "Get our money's worth outta ya. What's ya name?"

"Go by Hall; name's Robbie."

"Hall. This your dog?"

"Ozzie." He nodded.

"Good with cattle?"

"Yeah, he's more of a pet though."

"Well, he can bunk in the bunkhouse with ya; the lads'll enjoy having a dog around again. Trev, the old owner's lad, had him a mutt."

Robbie just nodded.

Carl patted Robbie's back. "I'll leave you to get acquainted. Edwards is in charge; he'll organize your hours and your pay. We've increased all the salaries; old man drove his men hard and paid them peanuts. Can't get good work out of men if you do that. We'll be in the front house. Sam and his family in the other over yonder." Carl gestured to the two large homes. "We expect all our men to attend church Sundays when not on shift. Edwards will see to it that everyone gets time off when needed."

"Thank you. I appreciate it." Robbie nodded to Carl and Samuel.

"Think nothing of it, Lad. Happy to give you a job. Work hard, be honest, and love the Lord. That's all we require of ya."

"Thank you. I will."

Carl and Samuel nodded and joined their families back in the wagons to head for their homes at last.

Edwards turned to Robbie. "Come on. I'll show ya where to put ya things."

Robbie and Ozzie followed him into a large bunk room. There were eight beds in the room, four on each side. At the end of the room was a pot-bellied stove in a small kitchen. A large table ran up between the beds. In one corner were two small couches and a table in between, scuffed from the spurs of many boots. The other corner had a coat rack with a line of boots below it. Each bed had a trunk at the end of it.

Three men were playing cards and eating steaming bowls of stew, a cup of coffee next to each.

Edwards greeted them. "Chaps, got a new man."

The three lay down their cards and stood.

"This is Robbie Hall. New boss brought him here."

Robbie nodded to the men and swallowed. The room reminded him of the orphanage with its rows of beds.

A man walked up to him and shook his hand. "Jerry Anders."

Robbie nodded to him.

"Marty Gray – everyone calls me Cook on account of I'm the cook." He chuckled.

Robbie smiled and nodded.

"Ollie Price." The youngest of the three greeted him.

"There are two others. Flynn and Lloyd, they're out on watch tonight. You'll meet 'em later. This is your bed, and trunk here. Just keep the place tidy, keep outta other people's things, and no liquor on site. We have two men at least out on the range all the time watching over the herd. Otherwise, there's plenty of work to do around the spread. They got some dairy animals too, and a few chickens. Boss plans to breed horses too."

Robbie nodded; it was a lot to take in.

"You take the weekend to get used to the place. You'll need to go to the store and get boots and chaps, book it to the ranch, and we'll dock your wages till it's paid off. Wage is a dollar a week, plus your food provided."

"Thank you." Robbie swallowed. It was rather overwhelming. He'd never been welcomed like this before, never had an actual job, just bits of work here and there wherever he could scrounge it.

"I'll leave you chaps to it." Edwards nodded to the men and began to leave.

"You don't live here?"

"Nah, got me a Mrs. We live in the cottage out back there. I'd better be getting back to her; I done enough hours for one day."

Robbie dumped his bag on his bed and nodded. "Much obliged."

Edwards nodded and walked out.

"Care to join us, Hall? You want some stew?" Cook offered.

"Thank you." Robbie took a seat and Cook thrust a bowl and spoon before him and a cup of hot coffee.

"Where you from, Hall?" Ollie picked up his cards and selected the one he wanted to play.

"Here and there." Robbie shrugged. Cook placed a bowl on the ground for the dog and resumed his spot at the table.

"Ya ain't got a home?" Jerry raised a brow and placed a card on top of Ollie's.

"Nah, grew up in an orphanage, been wandering for years."

"You gonna stay put now?" Cook lit a cigarette and put it in his mouth.

Robbie shrugged. "Maybe. Been looking for a place to call home."

"This is as good a place as any. Best job I ever had," Jerry offered. "Worked four other ranches 'fore I came 'ere. Never had a boss like these'n's. Better'n the previous chap. Baker and Turner is generous, 'spect ya to work hard and won't abide no slackers, but they's good to ya. Course they was only here for a few months 'fore they fetched their families, but they're decent. Last man was a bully."

Ollie grinned and slammed a card down. The others groaned and thrust their hands down in defeat. "I agree. It's a good job and Edwards is fair. Don't mess with 'im though; he can get onery sometimes. His Mrs. is as sweet as pie though. She brings us baking and mends our clothes for us. Almost like having a ma again." Ollie chuckled, gesturing to Robbie with the deck before he redealt the cards.

Robbie nodded and shrugged. "Wouldn't know. Never had a ma."

"Well, good to have you on board. You'll get to know the place in no time." Cook flicked his cigarette twice into the ashtray and reached for his cards. He glanced at them and masked his displeasure.

Three

"Aunty, I need to go town, you want anything?" Sadie put away the last dish.

"I'll come with you if I may. Shall we get coffee at the café too?"

"I'd love that; we haven't been out for so long."

Beth shook her head. "You do exaggerate. We went to the service on Sunday. That was only a few days ago."

Sadie wiped her cloth over the counters and rolled her eyes. "It feels like such a long time! I don't like being cooped up inside all day."

"No one said you had to be cooped up all day. I'm not old, and I don't need you to look after me. Go out and have fun. You're a young woman, and you ought to be enjoying yourself."

The two women removed their aprons and fetched their shawls from the hook. Sadie scooped up her basket and opened the door. "That sounds like the voice of experience, Aunty Beth. Did you enjoy yourself when you were a girl?"

"I sure did. Your uncle and I went to town dances and had a wonderful time back east, before the war."

Sadie shuddered. The war had taken her entire family when she was just a year old. Her Uncle and Aunt had taken her in and headed west to find a safer place to live. They'd built a house in a small Colorado town, and Uncle Jack ran the livery. The couple had no children, but they doted on Sadie and loved her as their own.

"It's a beautiful day." Sadie pushed back her bonnet as they walked.

"Yes, summer in Colorado sure is different than Virginia."

Sadie shrugged. "I don't remember. I was just a baby."

Beth nodded. Jack was in the corral outside the livery leaning against a large quarterhorse, the big hoof on his knee running a file across it. He saw the two women and grinned, put the hoof down, and walked up to the fence. "Hello, beautiful ladies."

"Hi, Uncle Jack." Sadie grinned.

The man smiled. His two women were his pride and joy. He stretched his back and removed his hat, running his fingers through his hair. "Just out enjoying the sunshine?"

Sadie lifted her basket. "Going to the store. Thought I'd make you a pie for supper."

Jack grinned widely. "Apple and cinnamon?"

"Of course." Sadie chuckled.

"Can't wait, Darling." He winked at her.

"We're gonna get some coffee at the café too," Beth added.

Jack put his hand out to her. "That's good. You've both been working hard, taking in sewing and the housework. It's nice to see you both having a break. I wish you didn't have to work." He grimaced.

"Now, Jack, we want to work and help out. I've always worked hard."

"I know. I had hoped to spare you that. I'm sorry I don't make more."

"Hush, Husband. I would've wanted to work no matter how much you made. I don't like sitting around doing nothing."

Jack leaned over the fence and kissed his wife's cheek. "You're a heck of a woman, Elizabeth Nelson. Sure am glad I married you nineteen years ago."

"Me too. Now you'd best get back to work. That horse isn't going to shoe itself."

He winked. "Yes, Ma'am." He nodded to them both, shoved his hat back on his head, and turned back to the horse.

"Come on, Dear, let's get our shopping done so we can have coffee. I need to get Mrs. Graham's dress finished this afternoon."

Sadie grinned and they hurried away.

"Good day, Mrs. and Miss Nelson." Geoffrey Weaver nodded as they entered the store.

"Mr. Weaver." Sadie grinned. They hurried to get their shopping done.

Three men walked in, and Sadie's cheeks reddened as she caught the eye of Lloyd Wood and Ollie Price. She had a shameless crush on Ollie. Before she turned down an aisle, she noticed a new man with them. A very handsome man. He was head and shoulders taller than Ollie, had a square jaw, and determined, piercing blue eyes. She noticed him command a dog to heel on the stairs as he walked in. She grimaced at the dog and turned back to look at the man. *He's right handsome, even more handsome than Ollie.* She hurried to catch up with her aunt.

"Gentlemen, can I help you?"

"Need to get young Robbie here looking like a real cowpoke." Lloyd whacked Robbie on the back.

Robbie sniggered. He really didn't like a fuss being made of him. "Just need some chaps and new boots." He lifted his foot and let the sole of the boot drop open. The store owner nodded and motioned them all to the storage area at the back of the shop.

Beth dropped the apple she held back into the produce bin and snapped her head up. She gasped and her eyes grew wide.

"What is it, Aunty?" Sadie touched her arm.

Beth chuckled. "Nothing, just thought that voice sounded familiar."

Sadie shrugged and they headed to the back corner to get their spices. She noticed the three cowboys follow the store owner into the back room.

They finished their shopping and the store clerk served them. Sadie tried to crane her neck to get a glimpse of Ollie, but she could only see his back and his sandy blonde hair. She grinned. *He's right handsome, too.*

*   *   *   *

"What would you like?" Gemma stood in front of the table in her starched apron.

"Coffee and muffins, please," Sadie spoke on their behalf.

"Certainly." The young woman hurried away through the swinging door into the kitchen.

"How much have you got left to do on the dress for Mrs. Graham?"

Beth looked at Sadie. "I have it cut out and ready. I'll get on the machine this afternoon, and I should be able to get it finished enough for her to try on tomorrow."

"You're such a talented seamstress, Aunty."

"I've always loved to sew. Of course it helps now that I have a machi... ahhhhhh." Beth gasped loudly and all the color drained from her face. She raised a hand to her mouth.

Sadie frowned and followed her aunt's gaze out the window. The three cowboys mounted their horses and galloped out of town. She turned to look at her aunt. Beth had wide eyes and her mouth dropped open. "What is it? You look like you've seen a ghost?"

Beth shook her head. "I think I did. Of course, it's not possible."

Sadie raised her brows. "What's not possible?"

Beth nodded her thanks to Gemma, who placed down two cups of coffee and two warm blueberry muffins. She turned to look at her niece. "Oh, it's nothing. I just thought I saw my brother. But of course, that's not possible. Ben died in the war." The woman laughed at her own silliness. "I imagine that new young cowboy just reminded me of him."

Sadie reached across and gripped her aunt's hand. A cloud washed over her and she shuddered. She gave the older woman a sad smile. "The war took so many good men."

Beth nodded. "It's been over fourteen years, and it still feels so close. I guess it touched everyone's lives in some way."

"Do you miss Virginia?" Sadie took a big bite of muffin.

"In a way."

"Did you ever think of going back?"

Beth shook her head and sipped at her coffee. "No, there are too many bad memories there. I lost my brother and his family, and you lost your family. Out here, we got a chance to start again and try to forget it ever happened."

Sadie nodded. "You've not told me much about your brother." She sipped at her own coffee.

Beth smiled. "Sergeant Benjamin Gordon. He was two years older than me. One of the youngest sergeants in the Confederate Army." Her voice gave away her pride in her brother. "We didn't find out for several years that he'd died. By that time, we'd taken you in and were living out here. We tried to write to find out what happened to his wife, but the only response we got was from an old church friend. She said all she knew was Pearl was at the camp visiting with Ben before he and the regiment were sent to battle. She was expecting at the time.

"When I wrote to the commanding officer, he sent a note saying as far as he knew, Pearl and the baby died in the infirmary."

Sadie squeezed her hand. "It seems there are so many stories like that. So many people who sent their men off to war and never saw them again. So many unaccounted for to this day. So much loss." Her voice trembled.

Beth nodded. "One good thing came from it."

Sadie frowned and tipped her head at her aunt.

Beth patted her niece's hand. "You came into our lives. Your Uncle Jack was only too happy to take in his brother's girl. He loved your father very much. It didn't make a shred of difference to him that they were both adopted. They were best friends and brothers. It broke Jack's heart when James died."

Sadie's lip trembled. "I wish I knew them. It was so horrible what happened."

Beth squeezed her hand. "Many homes were raided and people killed. Much evil took place during that battle, and our nation will take generations to recover. But I'm glad you were spared. Your mother hid you in her armoire when the soldiers came. She was very brave."

"I remember you telling me." Sadie drained her cup. "Uncle Jack found me screaming and trapped inside. He was flabbergasted they hadn't burned the house. They burned everything else."

"God's providence, Darling. He wanted you to live, and so you did."

Sadie nodded and tears flooded her eyes. "I know, Aunty, but I don't understand why he took my parents and my older sister." She closed her eyes. "In such a horrible way."

Beth squeezed both of Sadie's hands and the young woman raised sad eyes to her aunt.

"Dear, we mustn't question God and what He allows. Jack told me your father and mother were devout believers. God took them and your sister Elsie to be with Him. Just like He took my brother and his family and so many other families. But He also brought good from the war. Our country has changed for the better in many ways, and we got you. Let's not dwell anymore on what we lost and instead, celebrate His blessings. You got to grow up as a happy and healthy young woman, and your parent's legacy will continue through you."

"Thanks, Aunty. You and Uncle Jack have given me a wonderful life."

Beth grinned. "And I can't wait to see who you become, my dear. Now let's change the subject. It's your birthday in a few weeks. What shall we do to celebrate?"

"I dunno." Sadie shrugged. "Nothing special I don't suppose. We could just take a ride in the countryside and have a picnic."

"You don't want a big party? You only turn eighteen once."

Sadie frowned. "No, I don't think so. Most of my friends from school have left town or are already married. It'll just remind me that I don't even have a beau or any life prospects."

Beth patted her hand. "You will in time, Dear."

"Nah, I'm too wild for most men. Pretty enough, I guess, but I can never keep my dress clean or my hair in place or my temper down." Sadie grimaced.

Beth smiled at her. "And we wouldn't have you any other way. God made Sadie Nelson just the way you are, and He'll bring along the man for you when He's good and ready. We can't rush these things."

Sadie stood up and walked around the table to wrap her arms around her aunt. "Thank you, Aunty. I love you so much."

Beth kissed her hair. "And your uncle and I love you very much. God took such a tragic situation and made something good of it. We got to be parents; you got a loving home with family who love you."

Sadie stood and her aunt joined her. They paid for their meal and hurried home.

Four

Samuel Turner sat up in the saddle and looked across the herd. He nodded to the two cowboys headed back in at shift change. "You've done a good job, Robbie, settled in well, I hear."

"Thank you, Sir. I'm enjoying the work. I appreciate you taking the chance on me."

"We don't regret it. Edwards said you've fit right in and are hard working. It's all we can ask."

"You've been very generous. I appreciate you helping me out with the gear I need."

"It's not a problem, you need the gear, and you're paying for it anyway."

"Yeah, and I'm gonna have to get some new clothes, too. I don't have but two sets of clothing, and I need something for church. I gotta get my own horse, too."

"There's no hurry for that. The ranch has plenty you can use."

"I appreciate that, Sir, but I really would like to get my own. I've never had my own horse, and I'd sure like to."

"Tell, you what. You go choose your mount and we'll get it for ya. Just pay it off at ten cents a week."

Robbie grimaced. "That'll take months. I really should save for it."

"That will take just as long. How about this. I want to start breeding horses here on the ranch. Could use a man to help with that as a special project."

"Are you suggesting me?"

25

"Told me earlier you loved horses, and wanted to be a liveryman one day. I can see you're hard-working. I'd take ya on if you're keen to work with horses, 'stead a cows."

Robbie shrugged. "Don't know much about breeding horses. I like 'em plenty though."

"I do. Had a horse farm back in Kansas. I'd be happy to train ya up."

"What about riding the range? Edwards'll be a hand down."

"You'd still ride a few shifts with the herd, but the horses will keep us busy. I wanna start out with ten horses, and I might as well get eleven as ten. You help me do that, and we'll help you with the horse. Give it some thought. You've proven yourself to be a good man, and I feel like you're someone I can trust."

"I'm not sure how the other chaps will feel about that." Robbie grimaced.

"Edwards and I have already discussed a man for the horses. None of the others are interested."

Robbie raised his brows. "So, I'm your last resort."

"No, I just asked Edwards if the other men would have a problem with it. He asked them, and none were bothered. They're all happy riding the range."

"Well, I'm much obliged. I like working with horses. Worked in a few liveries in my time and I enjoyed them, 's'why I'd like to have my own one day."

Turner slapped his back. "Good. It'll come with a few perks too, like better hours, fewer night shifts, and we'll work towards a commission basis down the track."

"Commission?" Robbie squinted at his boss.

"Like when we sell up or you take 'em to market, you can have a percentage of the profit."

Robbie's brows flew up. "That's not necessary, Sir. A salary is all I need."

"It's common practice; that'll be down the track when we are established. In the meantime, go by the livery tomorrow and talk to the man there; see if he knows where we can get some good horses. See what 'e's got in stock, and if you like the look of 'em, get 'em."

"Yes, Sir. I sure will, first thing in the morning."

"Good, you can get yourself the new clothes you want too. You'll be dealing with buyers and sellers, so you need to look the part."

"You've made my day, Sir. Thank you for taking a chance on me; I won't let ya down. You know, I'm beginning to feel like God brought me here. He arranged for all this to work out."

Mr. Turner nodded. "He does that. Maybe you've found your home at last."

"I sure hope so, Sir. I've been roaming for far too long." Robbie sounded almost wistful.

The older man nodded and they went their separate ways around the herd.

* * * *

Sadie looked up from the kitchen when Jack walked in. "Uncle, you look exhausted."

Jack stretched his back and hung his hat on the hook. "I am. I'm just one man, and I'm struggling to keep up with the work."

"I could help. I like horses."

"There's more to my job than horses. And you're a lady; you don't need to be working in a livery."

"Uncle, I'm no delicate flower. I'd like to help. I could at least take care of the horses each day for you and ease your workload some. Please, I'd like to help."

"I'm not so sure. Aren't you needed around here?"

"It doesn't take two of us to run this small house. We've been taking in sewing mostly to pass the time."

Jack thought about it as he washed up and removed his boots. "I sure could use the help. You sure you could manage?"

"Course, I can manage."

"Very well, four hours a day, you can muck out and refresh all the stalls, exercise, groom and feed all the horses, even get 'em ready to shoe when needed."

Sadie grinned. "I'll start tomorrow."

Jack chuckled and sat down at the dining table at their bidding. "I'm looking forward to working with ya, Girl."

"Me too, Uncle. I'm a hard worker. I promise you won't regret it."

"I can't pay ya much."

"I don't want any payment. I just want to help you out."

"That's kind, Darling. But I want to pay you something."

"We'll work it out, Uncle Jack." She placed the last of the food on the table and they sat down to eat.

* * * *

"Stay, Boy." Robbie gestured to the dog to sit by the corral fence of the livery. Ozzie obeyed and sat back on his hind legs to wait. Robbie pushed open the gate of the livery corral and walked in.

"Hi there." Jack looked up. "You new to these parts?"

"Yep, working over the Circle A."

"Very good. You here on behalf of Turner I suppose."

"Name's Hall. I'm starting with the horses with Mr. Turner. He asked me to talk to you about getting some horses."

"He said someone would be by. How many are you thinking?"

"Eleven to start with. Ten breeders and a good riding horse."

The man raised his brows.

"I need a good saddle horse, too. Mr. Turner has agreed to make it part of my salary."

"Very good."

"Do you have any?"

"I've only got four for sale; the rest are hire horses or belong to others in town. I can get you more though."

"Mr. Turner wants good breeding horses, with pedigree preferred."

"I understand. Come and have a look at what I've got, and we can talk about getting what you need."

"I appreciate it, Sir." Robbie followed Jack inside.

Sadie walked toward the livery whistling to herself. She was really looking forward to working with her uncle, and she had always loved horses. Approaching the livery, she sucked in a breath and stopped. There was a dog out front. She'd been chased by a dog as a girl and had always had an irrational fear of them. "What is he doing there?" She trembled and inched slowly toward him.

Ozzie saw a potential friend and moved toward her. She gasped again and stopped walking. The dog kept moving. She turned and ran away; Ozzie thought it was a game and chased her. She screamed and ran in zigzags up the street, with the dog yapping at her heels.

Jack's head snapped up, and Robbie exclaimed, "What on earth?" Both looked at each other and hurried out to see what the noise was.

Robbie grimaced. He noticed the girl screeching with her hands in the air and Ozzie close behind, barking. He watched on in horror as the dog ran ahead of her, darted in front, and she fell over the dog and sprawled on the dust. "Ozzie, heel," he growled at the excitable pooch.

The dog slowed down and looked around. He reluctantly stopped and slunk his way over to his master. Robbie scolded him and told him to stay. He hurried over to Sadie. "I'm sorry, Ma'am." He put a hand out to help her up, but she pushed him away.

Sitting up in the dusty street, Sadie crossed her arms over her chest and scowled. "That your dog?"

"Yes, and I'm sorry. He gets a little carried away at times."

She stood up and thrust her hands on her hips. "You ought to put that mutt down, chasing people like that. You should be ashamed."

Jack watched from the corral and chuckled. Sadie didn't need his help.

"You ought to know better than to run from a dog. He thinks it's a game. Chase is one of his favorite games."

Sadie fixed her dark eyes on his and scowled. "Shame on you. That's no way to treat a lady."

Robbie shrugged. "Weren't me, was my dog."

Sadie began to calm down. "Next time, put that mutt on a leash. What's it doing at my uncle's livery in the first place?"

Robbie grinned. This was one fiery woman. He noticed the pins in her hair had worked loose and some of her dark hair hung long down her back. It was a rather beautiful brown, with just a touch of red through it. "He's with me. I've got business with your uncle." He smiled kindly. "I really am sorry. He's a good dog really."

Sadie squinted at him. "I never really liked dogs. I was chased by one as a child…"

Robbie chuckled slightly. "And again as an adult."

"You think it's a joke?" She screwed her face up at him. "Now, if you don't mind moving the filthy mutt so I can go to work."

He raised his brows.

"I work with my uncle at the livery, least I will be from today."

"Come over and meet Ozzie; he won't hurt you. You'll never get over your fear of dogs if you don't confront it."

"I never said I was afraid." She thrust her hands on her hips.

Robbie thrust his chin out and raised his brows. "Your eyes say it. Come on. He won't hurt you." He gestured to the dog, walked over, and squatted next to Ozzie. He tapped him on the snout and rubbed his ears.

Cringing internally, Sadie gingerly walked up to him. She refused to let this man see any weakness. "You'll hold him?"

"I've got him. He's not going anywhere. Just pet his head; he likes it."

Sadie bit her lip and reached a hand out towards the dog. She breathed loudly and a small squeal escaped her lips.

"It's okay, Miss; he won't hurt you." Robbie stroked the dog's head. Ozzie sat back on his haunches and dropped his pink tongue out the side of his mouth.

Sadie's lip trembled but she laid her hand on the dog's head.

"There see. He likes you." Robbie grinned as Ozzie nuzzled against her hand.

Sadie stood back up and breathed out. She nodded and marched into the livery.

Robbie chuckled and shook his head. "Stay." He growled at the dog. Ozzie whimpered and laid down, putting his head on his paws. "Good Boy." Robbie stroked his head and hurried back into the livery.

While he talked with Jack and inspected horses, he watched as Sadie led a horse out of the stall, tied it to the rail with a bucket of chaff, then picked up a pitchfork and went to work cleaning out the stall with gusto. He laughed internally. She was determined to not make eye contact with him.

*   *   *   *

Robbie rode the handsome quarterhorse towards the ranch, leading three more behind him.

Turner met him as he pulled up outside the corral. He walked around inspecting the four horses. "These are nice horses. You did well." He stroked the neck of the horse Robbie was riding. "Is this one the one you want as a saddle horse?"

"If that suits you, Sir?"

Turner petted the horse. "Yeah, he's a beauty."

"Name's Comet."

"You chose well. These other three are good horses too. It's a good start." Carl petted one on the rump.

"Mr. Nelson said he can get us more. He's got contacts all over the place. I went ahead and told him to make contact and let us know the prices."

"Good, taking initiative, I like that. Come on, let's get these horses into the corral."

Robbie nodded and followed his boss.

"You can put your horse in the stables with the ranch horses."

Robbie nodded again. "Thank you, Sir."

<h1 style="text-align:center">Five</h1>

Robbie sat up in his bed, leaning against the wall. Ozzie lay across his knee, and he stroked the dog's soft fur. He looked around at the three sleeping men. Jerry and Marty were out with the cattle, but the other three slept soundly. The various snores made a cacophonic symphony.

He'd been in Dusty Ridge two weeks so far and had got to know the town pretty well. He enjoyed the varied life on the range. Carl Baker and Samuel Turner turned out to be good bosses, and he liked the other cowboys he worked with, and working with the horses.

"What do you think? Could we make this our home, Oz?" he whispered and shrugged. "Home. What does that even mean?" He shook his head and closed his eyes. He'd never had a home or a family. The closest he'd come to family was his best friend, Timothy. They'd been as close as brothers ever could be. He'd got on well with the other children in the orphanage, but every time he'd befriend someone, they'd get adopted. He shrugged and ran his fingers through his hair. "But no one wanted me." He remembered watching as couple after couple came and adopted the children. He was even taken on an orphan train to various towns with eight other children. Everyone had been adopted except for he and Timothy, so they'd stuck together and became each other's family.

But now Timothy had his own family, and Robbie was all alone again. He shrugged. "I'm used to it. I guess I always will be alone unless God has other plans for me. But maybe at least this is a place I could belong."

His greatest desire in life was to have a home and a family, although he didn't think he'd be any good as a father. He didn't have the first clue about how to look after a child. He'd been raised with kindness and love by the pastor and Mrs. Bonnie. They never had any children of their own and just wanted to love all of God's children.

He smiled as he thought about 'Mrs. Bonnie' as they all called her. She really did love them. He remembered all climbing onto the sofa and listening to the pastor read the Bible. He remembered Mrs. Bonnie staying up with him when he was sick or climbing up on his bed to stroke his back when he'd had a bad dream.

She was the reason he'd grown up with love in his heart. He could've been an angry and bitter child, but Mrs. Bonnie and the pastor had taught them there was no point in being angry about things they couldn't change, to trust God with the circumstances, and do their utmost to live for Him every day.

I want to live for You, God. I'm not sure I really know how. I've searched for a home for so long. But Mrs. Bonnie was right. I have to live for each day.

He was sad to leave the only parents he'd ever known, but he and Timothy were young men, and they needed to go and make their way in the world.

The pastor and Mrs. Bonnie gave them their blessing and five dollars each. Robbie knew it was more than they could afford, but they insisted they take it and make something of themselves. Mrs. Bonnie asked them to write; when he was with Timothy, they'd sent a few letters back to the orphanage and even received one back when they were both in Colorado Springs. Even after six years, she was delighted to hear they were doing well. She included another five dollars in the letter and sent their blessings.

Robbie smiled as he remembered Timothy reading out the woman's response. The pastor had died a few years earlier, but still, she carried on in their ministry of love.

What makes people like that? What makes them give all they have to others and love so fiercely? He'd seen it in the two families who ran the Circle A. A real love and joy. They were fairly well off, not rich but comfortable, and they were generous and worked hard. Both Baker and Turner worked alongside the cowboys, and there wasn't a job they weren't prepared to do. Both took their fair share of shifts watching the cattle.

They'd invited the cowboys for a meal, and Robbie had enjoyed watching the children run around with Ozzie. The dog loved children and seemed sad when he had to leave. Robbie grinned. "Yeah, I think we could find a home here, Oz. It's the nicest place we've lived since leaving Mrs. Bonnie, and the best job we've ever had."

His mind turned to the incident at the livery. He couldn't help but chuckle out loud at the girl who had tripped over Ozzie. He had no idea who she was except that the man at the livery was her uncle. She had some spunk though. She certainly was no damsel in distress. He did feel some remorse that Ozzie had frightened her, but then she'd held her own just fine, and he was impressed she'd conquered that fear and stroked the dog.

He pictured her when she stood up after she'd fallen, hair all disheveled and dirt all over her skirts and even on her cheek. Her face curled up in fury. "She's a pretty tough girl, Oz."

The dog gave him two small whines and Robbie stroked his fur. He shuffled down the bed and found a comfortable position which he hoped would induce sleep. Ozzie laid his head on Robbie's chest.

*　*　*　*

"Hey, Hall, wanna come to town with us?"

Robbie gave his dog one more pet and stood up to look at Lloyd. "What ya thinking?"

"Got the whole day off, thought we might go and get some supplies at the store, spend some time at the saloon, and catch a meal at the café."

"I'll come, but I don't drink alcohol." He shuddered. He'd seen first-hand how much damage it could do.

"Please yourself."

"I need to get some clothes. Gotta have something decent to wear to church."

"The mercantile carries a range of things. Come on, let's go. Bring the dog if ya want."

Robbie thought about the last time he took Ozzie to town. "No, I think I'll leave him here."

"I'll watch him." Cook looked up from stirring the stew.

"Thanks, Cook. He's still got a sore paw, so don't let him out for too long."

Cook gave him a nod and reached for a carrot to peel.

The men hurried out to saddle their horses.

"He's a good-looking horse, Rob."

Robbie mounted the horse and patted his silky neck. "Yeah, he's a fine horse, aren't you, Comet?"

Lloyd raised his brows as he climbed up on his own horse. "What kinda name is Comet?"

"He's fast, like a speeding comet."

"If you say so." Jerry laughed. "We'll see who's fastest." He clucked to his horse, Jim, and galloped off.

Robbie and Lloyd looked at each other and grinned. "Come on, Comet." Robbie took off.

"Hey, wait for me." Lloyd nudged his horse, Ranger, and sped off after them.

The cowboys raced into town and arrived around the same time. The horses were relieved to stop; their sides heaved with exertion. The men dismounted, and the equines dumped their noses straight into the water trough. Robbie stroked his horse's neck. "Good job, Comet."

"Well, I'll see you chaps at the café." Lloyd turned and sauntered away with a wry grin on his face.

"Sure." Robbie shrugged. He turned to look at Jerry. "Where's he off to in such a hurry?"

Jerry grinned. "Got him a pretty girl."

Robbie raised his brows. "I wondered why he put on cologne just to come to town with us."

"He's got it bad."

Robbie looked almost wistful. "I envy him."

Jerry tilted his head to the side. "You looking for a girl?"

Robbie shrugged. "Some day. I never had a family. Sure would be nice to not spend my days alone."

Jerry raised his brows. "You got us!"

"Yeah, a bunch of smelly cowpokes wasn't really what I had in mind." Robbie screwed up his nose.

"I hate to tell you this, Hall, but you don't smell so great yourself after a day in the saddle."

Robbie chuckled. "Guess I'll have to work on that before I find a lady."

Jerry shook his head and they walked toward the mercantile. "There's a pretty girl." Jerry gestured with his head to Sadie walking out of the store.

Robbie grimaced.

Jerry frowned at him. "You don't think she's pretty?"

The younger man's lips twitched into a grin. "I think she's beautiful. I just had a run-in with her yesterday, and she's got a temper.... Ohhh." Robbie took off at a run.

Jerry frowned and watched on.

Sadie stepped out of the mercantile carrying a basket full of goods. Her head snapped around and she called back into the store at her friend, her face curled up in laughter. At the same time, she took a step and miscalculated, twisting her ankle roughly and ending up sprawled on the ground, some of her groceries lying on the dirt all around.

Robbie ran to her and knelt down. "Are you okay?" He put a hand on her shoulder.

"I'm just fine." She grimaced; there was no way she was going to be beholden to him. She began to stand up, but putting weight on her twisted ankle, she grimaced and fell back down.

"Please, let me help you?"

She sat up and thrust her hands over her chest. "No. I don't need your help."

He picked up all her groceries and shoved them in her basket. Placing it next to her, he knelt and put a hand on her arm. "You can't walk on that ankle. Please let me help you to the doc?" He looked up the street toward the infirmary.

"No. I'd rather sit here and never walk again than be beholden to the likes of you."

"You won't be beholden to anyone." He put his arm around her and slipped the other under her legs and scooped her up.

"Stop, put me down. Put me down!" She punched at his arms.

Robbie grimaced, the girl could really hit. He ignored the pain and walked down the street. Bystanders turned to watch.

Jerry chuckled, picked up her basket, and followed.

"Let me go. Put me down." She continued to yell and lash out at Robbie as he walked through the door of the infirmary. The doctor looked up from his journal and gasped; he thrust it down on the desk and jumped up, gesturing to the nearest bed.

Robbie laid her down and stood back.

"I said I didn't need your help. I'm fine." Sadie swung around and climbed off the bed, whimpered as she stood on her sore foot and collapsed to the floor.

Robbie shook his head, picked her up again, and placed her back onto the bed. "Just let the doctor look at your foot, Ma'am."

She scowled and thrust her arms over her chest again, and her lip trembled as anger radiated through her.

The doctor put a hand on her shoulder. "Miss Nelson, you need to lie back so I can look at your ankle."

She nodded, shot Robbie a glare and scowled. "You can leave now. I'm not a damsel in distress you need to rescue."

"I never said you were. I hope your ankle heals quickly." Robbie turned and walked out. Jerry put her basket on the counter nearby and followed him out.

"What do you make of that?" Jerry shook his head as they walked out into the sunshine.

"I told you she was feisty." Robbie grimaced.

"She's awful spunky alright; most women like a chivalrous gentleman."

Robbie scratched his jaw and shrugged. "She's definitely not, most women."

"Good luck to whatever man she ends up with. She's pretty, but that's too much spunk for me." Jerry shook his head.

"I agree." Robbie screwed up his face. "That's the second encounter I've had with her. Both have not gone well." The two cowboys walked toward the mercantile.

"Well, I doubt you'll have much to do with her. We don't get to town often, 'cept for church."

Robbie nodded. "Speaking of which. I need some new clothes."

"There you go, Miss Nelson. I don't believe it's a bad sprain, you just twisted it. Stay off it for a few days. Use the crutch to keep the weight off it when you do walk around."

"Yes, Doctor, thank you. I'm sorry for screaming when I came in here. That man makes me so angry."

Doctor Chapman sat back against the second bed and folded his arms over his chest. "Why?"

"Yesterday, his dog chased me up the street, and he seemed to think it was awful funny, and now this."

"Did he do this to you?" The doctor's face fell.

"No. I fell."

Tilting his head to the side and furrowing his brow, the doctor scratched at his chin. "Then why are you angry at him?"

"I told him I didn't need help. I could've got here just fine on my own." She thrust her arms over her chest and pursed her lips.

"Miss Nelson." The doctor stood up and placed a hand on her arm. "You couldn't walk. He was only doing what any man would do when they see a lady hurt. I don't think he had any ulterior motives."

She shrugged and pursed her lips out. "I despise being dependent on anyone."

The doctor frowned again. "Why? What's wrong with being dependent on someone?"

"Because I don't need his or anyone's help. I'm quite capable of looking after myself."

Doctor Chapman pulled up a chair and sat down. "You'll be alone all your life if you truly believe that."

"Why?"

"Because loving someone, whether that means a friend, a lover, or just an acquaintance, means being dependent on one another. The Bible is full of examples of people needing one another and commands us to love one another. I am fully dependent on my wife." He grinned and stroked his chin. "And she is fully dependent on me. I know she is quite capable of looking after herself, but why would you want that? I love it when Janie looks after me and when she allows herself to be vulnerable and trusts me to look after her. God made us that way, to need and rely on each other, be it a friendship or a relationship. If you stubbornly go through life determined you don't need anyone, then that's how you'll end up."

Sadie grimaced. She didn't say anything and still seethed internally.

The doctor put a hand on her shoulder. "Miss Nelson, there is nothing more beautiful than people depending on one another. My wife is so much stronger than me in so many ways, but the fact that she lets me do things for her, protect and serve her, is wonderful to me. I don't mean that she's a fragile little woman and I'm a big strong hero. I mean, she's so precious to me that I want to honor her and love her and do everything I can for her, not because she's weak, but because I love her and for no other reason."

"I don't love that man. I don't even know his name."

"No, me either. I believe he's a new cowboy over at the Circle A ranch. Still, don't shun his kindness. He wasn't trying to undermine you."

"I guess." She exhaled.

"That's a girl. Now, how are we going to get you home, Missy?"

"I can walk." She grinned at him.

The doctor's eyebrows flew up. "Nice try. Stay here. I'll go fetch your uncle. Do not leave that bed young lady, or I'll send that cowboy back in here to carry you home in his arms."

Sadie screwed her face up at the doctor in mock hurt and nodded. He chuckled and hurried out the door, returning right away with Jack.

"Oh, Sadie, Darling, what've you done?"

"I fell, Uncle, and twisted my ankle. I'll be fine in a few days."

"Come on, let me take you home." He put an arm around her and the other under her legs, and she put her arms around his neck.

Looking up at the doctor with a grin, she turned back to her uncle. "Thank you, Uncle. I need help getting home. I can't walk."

"Just hold on, Sweet Girl. I'll get you there in a jiffy." Jack looked at the doctor. "Much obliged for you taking care of my girl, Doc. I'll be by to fix up the bill later."

The doctor nodded. "No rush, Jack, just what you can when you can, as always."

"I appreciate it." Jack walked out the door.

The two cowboys were sitting at a table outside the café when Jack walked out with Sadie in his arms. Robbie jumped up and walked over. Sadie scowled at him.

"I just want to say sorry if I over-stepped my bounds, Ma'am. I wasn't about to leave you in the street hurt."

She looked at Robbie and gave him a single nod, the doctor's words still ringing in her ears. She wasn't about to forgive him, and she hoped she never had to see him again. That would be just fine by her.

Robbie nodded and hurried back to Jerry.

"Why'd you apologize? Weren't you who had a fit."

"Because she was upset."

"Why do you care? You don't even know her name."

"The Good Book says to love your neighbor. The pastor that raised me taught us that." He shrugged.

The slightest blush on Robbie's cheeks caused Jerry to nod and grin. Robbie watched until the girl was out of sight and then turned to walk back to the café.

Six

"You have everything ready?" Jack walked out into the kitchen in his Sunday shirt and trousers, his hair still wet at the front from washing his face.

"Yes, just the picnic basket and blanket." Sadie gestured to them sitting nearby.

"Great. Let's go, shall we?" He scooped up the basket and put his other arm out to his wife. "You look lovely today, Mrs. Nelson." He kissed her cheek. "I do so love you in yellow. Makes your lovely brown hair and eyes really stand out."

"Thank you, Dear."

He winked at Sadie as she picked up their Bible. "You look lovely, too, Sadie. Your new pink dress is quite becoming. I'll have to keep an eye on the young men." He gave her a mock growl.

"If only. Uncle Jack. No one seems interested in me." Sadie rolled her eyes and scowled.

Jack put down the basket and let go of his wife. He walked to Sadie and embraced her. Cradling her head against his chest, he kissed her hair. "That's because the Lord hasn't brought along the right fella yet. But you're a wonderful girl, and some young man is gonna steal you right out from under me." He pulled back and gripped her by both shoulders. "You're just like your ma, full of spunk and adventure. James fell head over heels for her from the moment he first laid eyes on her. Told me that very day he was gonna marry her."

"Really?"

"Really. He wasn't interested in the sweet, gentle girls, like my Beth." He winked at his wife. "He wanted a girl with some passion and fire, and boy, did he find her. They had some pretty fiery moments when they were courting, but he was so passionately in love with her. I've never seen a love like it. I remember him writing me when they found out about you. He was so thrilled I could feel the love on the pages. He told me he hoped you were a little girl just like her ma. He had one girl and hoped for another."

Sadie smiled and tears flooded her eyes. "You've never told me that before."

Jack regained the picnic basket and led them out. "He wrote me after you were born. It took a long time to get to us; the war made things difficult for the mail. He raved about you, how precious you were, and just how smitten he was by you. I'm confident in time, you'll find just the right man, Darling." He furrowed his brow. "He'll have to be a good man to be worthy of my Sadie. And on that day, I'll be sorry to give you up."

Sadie gripped her uncle's arm, the one that held the basket. "Thank you, Uncle Jack. I'll be sorry to leave you both."

"I know, but it's right. It's how it's meant to be." He led them up the stairs to the church, just as the opening hymn was being sung. They grimaced at their lateness, stowed their basket and blanket under the seat, and stood to join in the song.

When the service finished, people began chatting and collecting their things for the town picnic in the common next to the church. Some stopped to chat for a moment.

From their seat near the back, Beth could hear their young Pastor Kelley and his wife Tina talking to each person as they always did, with loving-kindness. They really loved their congregation and took pastoral care seriously.

The Nelsons were deep in conversation with the Vickorys sitting across the aisle when Beth heard that voice again. She swiveled around to look where it had come from and gasped loudly. Immediately collapsing onto the floor in shock.

"Beth." Jack hovered over her. "Doc," he yelled to Doctor Chapman across the room. The man came running over and knelt before the woman as she came to. All conversation stopped and heads turned to watch.

"Mrs. Nelson, can you hear me?"

"Yes." The woman gripped her head as her foggy brain registered the situation. "I'm fine."

Jack and the doctor helped her back to her seat. "What happened?" The doctor observed her with his eyes.

"I saw a ghost."

"What do you mean?" Jack frowned.

She turned and stood up and looked right into the dazzling blue eyes of her brother. "Benjamin?" She frowned and put a hand out to the man.

Robbie frowned and looked at her. "No, Ma'am. I believe you're mistaken. My name's Robert."

Sadie scowled at the man and her cheeks colored deeply. He was the last person she wanted to see.

Beth walked up to Robbie, her eyes glistening. "You look exactly like my brother, Benjamin Gordon."

Robbie shrugged. "I don't know what to say, Ma'am. I'm much too young to be your brother."

"But you're the spitting image. Same eyes, same broad shoulders, and his square jaw. I'd recognize him anywhere. What's your last name and where are you from?"

Robbie shrugged. "I'm afraid I don't rightly know. I believe I was born in Virginia. I don't know my father's name. All I know about my identity is my mother was named Pearl, and I'm named for her father. Robbie Hall."

Beth's mouth fell open and she put a hand to her face. Tears flooded her eyes and she instinctively wrapped her arms around the man. "Oh, bless ya. Bless ya, Robbie. I thought you'd died."

Sadie grimaced and scowled at the man.

Robbie patted the woman on the back. He stepped back from her and frowned. "I don't understand. Do you know me?"

"I knew your parents." Her lips trembled.

Robbie gasped. "You did."

"Yes. Sergeant Benjamin and Pearl Gordon."

Robbie swallowed and reached into his pocket. He lifted out the small New Testament and slipped the photo out and passed it to her.

Sadie's eyes blazed and she gritted her teeth. *Why him? Why does it have to be him?* She thrust her hands on her hips and watched on, unable to shake the fear that this man was about to steal her family from her.

"Ohhhhhhh." Tears washed down Beth's cheeks. She touched the face of her brother in the photo and Jack shook his head.

Robbie frowned. "I don't understand."

Beth reached a hand up to place on the young man's cheek, she smiled through her tears. "You're my nephew. Sergeant Benjamin Gordon was my brother. He died in the war, at Manassas."

Robbie took a deep breath. He turned, hurried out of the church, ran down the stairs, and stood bent over with his hands on his knees, heaving in deep breaths. His mind was spinning. *All my life, all my years of roaming, all I ever wanted was a family.* But suddenly it felt overwhelming and somewhat scary.

Beth and Jack approached and Robbie stood upright. "Sorry for walking out. This is just a bit overwhelming."

Beth gripped his arms. "I completely understand. Oh, Robbie. You're the spitting image of your father, and I'm delighted to meet you. I was told you'd died."

"You knew about me?"

"I knew my brother's wife had died in childbirth, but I was told her child had died too. No one could give me much information, and I didn't even find out anything about my brother or Pearl 'til the war was nearly over. If I'd known you were alive, I would have scoured the country to find you." Tears rolled down her cheeks. "Oh, thank the Lord for bringing you here after all these years." She embraced him again.

Sadie pouted, dropped her head, and tried desperately to fight back the tears.

Robbie gulped and put his arms around the tiny woman. Unfamiliar feelings surged through him. *I actually have family.* He gulped over and over again.

Beth released him and took him by the hand. "Oh Robbie, you must join us for the picnic, I insist. I want to know all about you and how you came to be in Dusty Ridge, everything."

Sadie gritted her teeth and growled from deep in her throat. The last thing she wanted was to have to eat with that man, or have him eat the pie she made.

No one else even existed to Beth at that moment but her brother's boy. Robbie merely nodded and let her lead him to the picnic spot. Jack and Sadie followed. Sadie grimaced, her resentment toward him growing by the minute. Beth was her aunt, not his! Of course, she wasn't Beth's flesh and blood, and neither was she really Jack's. Both Jack and her father had been adopted, although it made not a scrap of difference, and they never even thought about it. They were just brothers, and that was that.

Sadie fumed internally. It wasn't fair. This was her aunt and uncle and hers alone! She didn't want to share them with the likes of him. She went along with it because it made her aunt happy, but that was the only reason. She would have lunch with him, but they couldn't force her to like him or his ugly mutt.

With a scowl, she spread out the picnic blanket and Beth gestured for Robbie to sit. He obliged and looked around at the other faces who sat with them.

"Robbie, this is my husband, Jack Nelson, and his niece, Sadie."

Robbie nodded to them both. What a turn of events. His aunt! And that girl, the beautiful, feisty young woman, was her husband's niece. Having a family was mystifying for him. He didn't know how to have family, but he sure was keen to learn. *It's all I ever wanted.* He shook Jack's hand. "We've met, of course."

"At the livery, didn't know then you were Beth's nephew." Jack chuckled. "It's a small world."

Robbie gave him a sideways smile. "Neither did I."

Sadie folded her arms across her chest and scowled at him. "Too small," she muttered.

"It's nice to meet you, Miss Nelson. Nice to know your name at last." Robbie smiled kindly. Sadie refused to make eye contact with him. She gritted her teeth and stared at the picnic basket.

He shook his head and turned to his aunt. "So, my name's Gordon?"

Sadie busied herself with dishing out the pie, giving Robbie the smallest piece on purpose. She didn't want to waste good pie on him.

"Yes. Your father was Benjamin Allen Gordon. He married Pearl a year before the war broke out. He'd been in the army for a time by then, and they found out about you six months before the war began. I know because he wrote to tell me. We were living in Western Virginia by then."

Robbie nodded. "I've gone twenty-one years not knowing who I am." He opened his mouth and sniffed back the rising emotion, swiping at his eyes.

Sadie scowled at him.

"Well, now you do, and you're so welcome, Robbie." Beth squeezed his hand. Her eyes sparkled in joy. "It's so wonderful to meet you. Oh, I can see my brother looking at me in your eyes." Her lips trembled.

"Thank you, Mrs. Nelson."

"Please, won't you call me Aunt Beth. It would make me most happy to have Ben's boy around. I insist you come to our home for supper. I want to get to know you. I do hope you plan to stay in this town for a time."

"Dunno." He shrugged. "Never really stayed in one place for long. Never had a place to call home."

Good. You can go right back to wherever it was you came from and leave my family alone. Sadie's lips pursed tightly and her brow furrowed. Deep brown eyes pierced his soul. He chuckled internally. "I'd like that, Aunt Beth."

A low groan emanated from Sadie and she busied herself tidying up, slamming the tin plates together loudly in the basket.

"Sadie. Take care," her aunt scolded.

Sadie just nodded, but the scowl didn't leave her face.

Seven

Beth hurried from the kitchen, discarding her apron as she ran to open the door. "Ohhh, Robbie, Dear, won't you please come in?"

Robbie nodded and swallowed nervously. The idea of 'family' was a foreign concept to him. "Thank you, Ma'am. I appreciate it."

"You don't have to call me, Ma'am, I'm just Aunt Beth. I know it'll take some getting used to, but you're our family, and you're welcome here."

A loud scoff came from the kitchen, and Sadie masked her anger by dropping a wooden spoon on the floor. Bending to pick it up, she scowled. *Why does it have to be him? Why does he get to take my family?*

Beth gripped Robbie's hand and led him to the living room. "Please sit down. Would you like some coffee?"

"Yes, thank you."

Aunt Beth looked up at the kitchen. "Sadie, Dear, could we all have some coffee?"

Sadie screwed up her face and seethed. *And now I have to serve him.* She thrust the coffeepot on the stove and slammed three cups on the counter. Aunt Beth looked up and shook her head.

Robbie swallowed over and over again and looked around nervously. Beth sat down next to him and patted his hand. "It's okay, Robbie. You don't have to be nervous. We're your family, and you're welcome here just the way you are."

He nodded and gave her a smile. "Sorry, Aunt Beth. I just never had a family before. I don't really know how I'm supposed to respond." He shrugged. "Been on my own for many years, with just my dog for company."

"Ohhhh." Beth lay her head against his shoulder and put an arm around him. "You've had such a hard life. I'm so sorry. If I'd known about you, I'd have come to find you and raised you in a house full of love."

"Oh, I was shown love, Aunty. I was luckier than most, Mrs. Bonnie, and her pastor husband were kind to us children in the orphanage. They did love us, but it wasn't the same as having a family."

Sadie walked over, a steely glare on her face. She thrust a cup out to Robbie, so forcefully that some of the liquid slopped over the side and onto his hand. "Here ya go," she grunted.

Robbie flinched as hot coffee hit his skin. He gave her a nod and took the cup, trying not to grimace. Sadie passed her aunt a cup too and hurried back to the kitchen.

Beth frowned at her as she wandered away. "Sadie, bring Robbie a cloth to wipe up."

Robbie meant to protest, but Beth insisted.

"Yes, Ma'am," Sadie muttered under her breath. *I'm nothing but a servant.* "Here." She threw the cloth across the room and Robbie caught it and wiped up the spill.

Sadie marched over, snatched her shawl off the hook, and opened the door.

"Where are you going, Sadie?" Beth frowned at her.

"To see if Uncle Jack needs any help with the firewood," she hissed through her teeth.

"He'll be fine, Dear. Why don't you come and join us?"

"No, I know when I'm not wanted." She gritted her teeth and stormed out the door.

"Sadie..." Beth called after her.

"I'm sorry, Aunt Beth. I've caused a rift. I'll go and leave you folks be." Robbie started to stand up.

Beth put a hand on his arm. "Nonsense. You're just a shock is all. Sadie's had us all to herself for many years, and she's not used to having to share. She'll come round."

"I hope so. I never wanted to come between you. She's your actual family. I've just arrived."

"And you've missed out on twenty-one years of a family's love." She squeezed his arm. "And I'm going to make up for that."

Robbie shook his head. "You don't have to. I'm fine on my own, Aunt Beth." He shrugged. "I've made it this far in life alone, it's just good to finally know who I am."

"Not anymore. Now we'll have no more arguments. You're my nephew, and I loved your father very much."

"What was he like?" Robbie heard himself asking, his swirling emotions causing the slightest tremor to his voice.

"Wait here. I've got something to show you."

Robbie nodded and sat drinking his coffee as she jumped up and hurried out of the room. She was soon back with a small case in her hands. She laid it on the coffee table. Robbie watched as she opened it.

She pulled out some photographs and flicked through them until she came to one from her childhood.

She held out the very faded and very tatty photograph to Robbie. "This is your father and I on my first day of school. He held my hand all the way, and I cried because I was so scared. I remember when he walked me to my classroom, he bent down to look at me and said, 'Bethy. We are Gordons, and Gordons are brave. No more tears. You walk in there with your head held high, just like Papa and Mama said. Be proud of who you are and take it all in your stride.' He hugged me and gave me this." She held up a shiny rock.

Robbie lifted his brows in question.

"This was his favorite rock. He loved to collect interesting rocks. See this one, with the yellow streak through it. He told me it was gold and would make whoever held it brave. He gave it to me and told me to keep it in my pocket. Whenever I felt afraid, I was to put my hand in my pocket, grip the rock and remember who I was."

Robbie nodded. "Sounds like he was a kind person."

"Yes, but he was also brave and strong." She flicked through and pulled out another photograph. "This was the day he was promoted to sergeant. Look how strong and brave he is. He had these broad shoulders and the same square jaw as you."

Robbie smiled and took the photo, holding it in his hand, he looked down at his own likeness, closed his eyes and sighed. "I wish I'd known them. I always felt like something was missing in my life."

"Do you have anything of theirs?"

Robbie nodded, reached into his top pocket, and pulled out the pocket watch, the New Testament, and his mother's rings and cameo she'd been wearing when he was born. "This is the sum total of all I have of theirs. I've carried them with me all my life." His voice trembled. He put the cameo and rings back in his pocket.

Beth's eyes filled with tears and she touched the pocket watch he held out. "May I?"

"Of course."

She took the watch and turned it over in her hands. She sighed deeply. "I remember the day Ben got this. He was heading off to the army, and Papa sat us both down and prayed with us, then lifted the pocket watch from his pocket and gave it to Ben. Papa was so proud of Ben, and so was I."

Robbie merely nodded. His lips trembled and he sniffed away tears. "Sorry," he apologized. "This is all just very overwhelming."

Beth squeezed his hand. "Of course, it is. There is no need for you to be sorry. It'll take time to adjust to having a family after being alone for so long."

"But it's all I ever wanted. A family, a home, a place to belong."

Beth grinned and patted his arm. "I hope you find it here. Find a good woman and settle down."

Robbie nodded. "I'd like that. I don't know if I'll ever be any good at being a husband or father. I'm so used to being alone I don't know if I can be dependent on someone else or have someone depend on me."

Beth patted his arm. "You'll be fine, Dear. You'll learn quickly."

At that moment, Jack and Sadie walked in with armloads of firewood. "Good evening, Robbie."

"Mr. Nelson." Robbie nodded. He gave Sadie a slight smile but was rewarded with a scowl. They discarded the wood into the box by the fireplace and Jack sat to join the conversation.

Sadie hurried to the kitchen, hoping to throw herself into making the meal and take her mind off that infernal man.

"So, how've you been settling in, Son?"

Sadie gasped at the familiar term Jack had used inadvertently. The potatoes had never been whipped more smoothly as she took her aggression out on them.

"Just fine, thank you. As you know, I'm getting to work with Mr. Turner and the horses."

"Are you enjoying that?"

"Yeah, it's a good job. I've always liked horses, worked in liveries and ranches at times."

"I could've done with a man like you to help around the livery."

Sadie gasped, dropped the pot of potatoes on the floor and strode into the living room, thrust her hands on her hips and scowled. "What's wrong with the help I give, Uncle? What, I'm not good enough because I'm a woman?"

Jack frowned. "Sadie, I'm not saying that. You know I appreciate your help."

Robbie stared at his coffee cup, unsure where else to look.

"Yeah, but you won't let me do certain things because you don't think I'm strong enough. Well, you needn't worry, you have a son now." She thrust her hand out at Robbie. "I guess I'm not needed anymore." Her lips trembled as she desperately held back the tears. She snatched her shawl from the hook and stormed out again, slamming the door behind her. Two framed pictures fell from the wall and broke on the floor, and one of the lower windowpanes smashed.

Robbie sighed. "I'm sorry. I should never've come here. I've ruined everything for you. Thank you for inviting me for supper and telling me about my family." He stood and strode to the door.

"Wait, Robbie, don't go." Beth ran to him and wrapped her arms around him. "Please don't leave."

He stepped back from her. "If this is what it's like having a family. I'm better off alone. I'll tell my boss I'll work out my notice." He choked. He loved his current job, it was the best situation he'd ever had, but he'd ruined a family without meaning to, and he had to get out of there. "And I'll leave town." He swiped at his eyes. "I won't disturb you again. Thank you for your kindness, and telling me who I am. I'm grateful to you for that."

"No, Robbie, please don't go." Beth clung to him.

Robbie's lip trembled and he pushed her from him, grabbed his coat and hat and strode out, jumped on Comet, and galloped away. Beth collapsed to the floor in sobs. Jack ran to her and held her. His mind racing. He knew he had to go find Sadie, but Beth needed him too.

Jack soothed her, and when she stopped crying, he pulled back from her. "I need to go and find Sadie. Are you going to be okay?"

"Yes. I'll stay back and pray. I've made an awful mess of things."

Jack pulled her close again. "No, you haven't. You've done nothing wrong. I understand how you feel about Robbie because that's how I felt about Sadie when we took her in, and I can't imagine what it's like having him come back from the dead like this. It'll all work out. You'll see."

She nodded against his chest. "I know. I'll be okay. Please find her, and somehow I have to find a way to make amends with Robbie. Now that I've found him, I can't lose him. Tell Sadie loving Robbie, doesn't mean I don't love her too."

"I will. She'll understand."

*　*　*　*

It took Jack more than an hour to find Sadie. He'd checked the livery several times, certain that was where she'd go. It wasn't until the third check that he found her in the hay loft sobbing, her head in her hands on her raised knees. He climbed up the ladder and sat next to her, put one arm around her, and held her while she sobbed. She didn't lean into him, but she didn't refuse him either.

When she finally stopped crying, she sat back from her uncle, unwilling to make eye contact. Jack still did not speak. He pulled out his handkerchief and offered it to her. She took it, wiped her eyes and blew her nose, then tucked it into her sleeve.

Jack reached over and lifted her chin. "Sadie, what's this all about?"

"Aunt Beth has Robbie now; and you can have the son you always wanted. You won't need me anymore."

Tears flooded Jack's eyes, and he sniffed loudly and sucked in a deep breath.

His emotion touched Sadie and it sobered her. "What is it?"

He swiped at his eyes. "How could you ever think that, Sadie?" He closed his eyes and brushed away another tear. "My darling girl. Even had I ten sons, I'd still want you very much and love you more than I can ever say. That is never going to change, Sweet Girl. If you really think that, then I've failed you as a father."

Sadie burst into tears and threw herself in his arms. He clung to her, laying his head on hers, he rocked back and forth, stroking her hair. "I love you, Sadie. You're my pride and joy, the apple of my eye."

"I love you, too," came her muffled voice. She sat back and wiped her eyes again.

"Won't you come on home?"

"Is HE still there?" Her lip trembled.

"No. Robbie left. He said he's going to leave town."

"Good."

"Sadie, you don't mean that."

"I do so." She thrust her arms across her chest and fire grew in her dark eyes.

"But why? What have you got against him?"

She wiped at her eyes. "He's going to take my family from me."

Jack closed his eyes. "Why would you say that?"

"Beth is my aunt, not his. Look how she's fawned over him since this morning. She's talked about nothing else all day and has barely even noticed me. I'm nothing but a servant girl to wait hand and foot on her precious Robbie. He's nothing but a loner and a drifter. I wish he would go away and leave my family alone."

"Sadie Nelson, that is not fair."

"It's how I feel. She loves him more than me. I can tell."

Jack hung his head for a moment. He looked up at her, his eyes filled with tears. He lifted a weathered hand and cupped her cheek. "Sadie, what if one day, your father or mother, or your sister, who'd been dead for twenty years, suddenly appeared in your life?"

She let out a sob and nodded. "I'm afraid if she has Robbie, she won't love me anymore. I'm not her flesh and blood, and now she has a real relative."

"Tell me this. If your father did turn up today, would you love me any less?"

Sadie snapped her head up to look at her uncle. "Of course not! Oh, Uncle, I'll always love you. You're the only father I've ever known."

"Yes, and Aunt Beth is the only mother you've ever known, and you are the only daughter she's ever known. She couldn't love you more if you'd been her flesh and blood. And let me assure you, Darling, blood has nothing to do with it. I loved your father as much as a person can love a brother, and we were not blood." He stroked her cheek and smiled at her. "Sadie, put yourself in Robbie's shoes, because you could very well have been him, so could I, and your father. Imagine if you'd not grown up with a family to love you. Imagine you'd spent your life in an orphanage. That man didn't even know his name until today. You've always known that you're a Nelson."

Sadie bit her lips together and grimaced, then let out a loud sigh. "You're right, Uncle. I just don't like him one bit, and the thought of Aunty Beth loving him made me angry."

"You know she can love both of you. But right now, this is new to your aunt. In a way, he's back from the dead, and the only piece of her brother. Imagine if it was you in her situation. You don't need to feel threatened by Robbie. In a way, he's your cousin."

She thrust her arms over her chest and scowled. "No, we are not related, he's not my cousin, and I don't like him."

"Whyever not? He seems personable enough. A bit aloof and uncertain, which is to be expected after the life he's led."

"His dog chased me, and he laughed, then he picked me up like a silly little girl and marched me into the clinic as though he was a brave knight rescuing a damsel in distress."

Jack shook his head. "You are your own worst enemy, Sadie Nelson."

"What do you mean?"

"You know full well it wasn't his fault that you're terrified of dogs, and he didn't laugh at you. He was genuinely concerned afterward. And if he hadn't carried you into the clinic, then you wouldn't have made it there. If you keep putting up these walls, you'll never let anyone in."

"What are you saying?"

"You told me no one could ever love you. If that's true, it's only you that's making it true." He smiled kindly and stroked her cheek. "There is nothing wrong with letting someone help you, of showing your tender heart and being vulnerable sometimes. It doesn't make you weak. Oh, Sadie, you have so much to offer, but if you keep these walls up, you'll end up alone, and I don't want to see that for you. I just want to see you happy."

Her lip trembled. "I'm afraid." She dropped her eyes.

"Afraid of what?"

"That if someone sees what I'm really like, they won't like me."

Jack lifted her chin so she'd look at him. "Sadie Nelson, that's garbage. You are so loveable. You're strong, stubborn, and tenacious, which I love about you, but I also love your softness, your sweetness, and your tender heart. With all you've been through, losing your family, you could well be bitter. Look how hurt and insecure Robbie is. He needs our love and support. Give him a chance. You never know; you might even come to love him someday."

"I'm not sure about love." She took a deep breath. "But I'll try."

"That's my girl. Now come on. Aunt Beth will be worried sick."

"I'm sorry, I got so defensive. You're right. It's not Robbie's fault. I just hate how foolish he makes me feel."

Jack helped her down the ladder and gave her his arm. "Foolish?"

"Whenever I'm around him, I feel all twisted up. Like I'm determined to show him I'm not a silly little girl, then I go do something like fall down the stairs and prove to him that's exactly what I am." She rolled her eyes.

"You're not foolish, and he doesn't think that. Now for Aunt Beth's sake, will you at least be civil? She deserves to get to know her nephew, don't you think?"

Sadie gave her uncle a shy smile. "Alright."

"That's my girl." Jack kissed her forehead and they headed for home.

Eight

Sadie ran in the door of the house to find Aunt Beth at the table with her hands over her face sobbing. "Oh." Sadie ran to her and fell into the chair next to her. "I'm sorry, Aunt Beth. I'm so sorry."

Beth embraced her, looked up, and wiped her eyes. "I'm sorry too, Darling. Sorry I made you feel like I didn't care." She smiled and reached up to tuck a loose strand of hair behind Sadie's ear. "I love you more than I could ever explain."

"I know, Aunt Beth. I'm sorry I let my insecurities get the better of me. There's something about him that drives me crazy, and the thought of him weaseling his way into our family made me cross. But I understand because if someone from my family came back from the dead like that, I'd hug them tight and never let them go."

"I feel for him, Sadie. He never got to have a loving family like you did."

Sadie embraced her aunt. "I know, and I'm ever so grateful to you. If you hadn't taken me in, I might have ended up in an orphanage too. Of course it's right that you love him. I'm sorry I was jealous."

"Oh, Sadie Girl. You have no reason to be sorry. I hope you and Robbie will grow to be close."

Sadie sat back and crossed her arms over her chest. "I promised Uncle Jack, I'd be civil to Robbie, but that's all I can promise."

Beth looked at her and the slight blush that grew on her cheeks and grinned. "Fair enough, Darling. That's all I ask for now."

"Is supper ruined?"

"No. Shall we eat?"

"What about Robbie? Uncle told me he left."

Aunt Beth's lip trembled. She swiped at her eyes with her handkerchief. "He said he's going to leave town. He doesn't like that he's caused a rift."

"Well, that's nonsense." Determined Sadie took over. "Tomorrow, I'm gonna march over to that ranch and tell him it's nonsense. He shouldn't miss out on a family because of me. I may not like him very much, but you don't deserve to miss out on getting to know him."

Jack walked in from stowing his horse and caught the end of the conversation. Beth flashed him a knowing grin. There was more to Sadie's outburst than the girl even knew.

*   *   *   *

Robbie rode the range looking out across the herd. He sighed loudly and stroked Comet's neck. He stopped his horse and removed his hat, running his fingers through his hair. Comet gave a snort in solidarity for his master's melancholy thoughts.

"I finally found a family, and all I've done is ruin it." He took a deep breath. "It seems everything I touch gets ruined. Perhaps I'm better off leaving town. Just being on my own." He sighed. He wasn't looking forward to telling his boss he needed to leave, but it was for the best. *God, I love this job. I love this town. It was beginning to feel like home. For the first time in my life, I've found family and a sense of belonging.* He ran his fingers through his hair again. *Maybe it's best I leave right now before I get too attached, and let the chips fall where they may.* He turned the horse and galloped back towards the bunkhouse.

"Hey, Robbie, where ya going?" Jerry yelled from the other side of the herd. He clucked to his horse and chased after Robbie. But the man galloped away. Jerry shrugged; he couldn't leave the herd, so he turned and went back to work. The shift would change in a few hours and he'd talk to Robbie then.

Robbie stormed into the bunkhouse and thrust open his trunk. He shoved everything into his knapsack.

"Hey, Hall, what's going on?"

He turned to look at Cook. "I'm leaving."

"What, why?" The cook screwed his face up.

Robbie shrugged. "Just time to leave. Already stayed here too long."

Flynn stood and crossed his arms. He squinted at Robbie. "What's going on? I thought you liked it here?"

"I do, it's the best job I ever had." Robbie's lips quivered. "I knew it was too good to be true."

"I don't understand." Lloyd was eating before he took the next shift. "If you like it so much, why leave?"

"Got my reasons. Tell the boss I'm sorry." He whistled to his dog.

"You at least gonna leave a note?" Cook asked.

"No. Just tell the boss I'll find a way to pay for the horse. I'll send money as soon as I can get another job. I won't be beholden to him." Robbie tried desperately to keep the tears at bay.

"Where will you go?" Cook frowned.

Robbie shrugged. "Dunno, back to roaming, I guess. Might go see my friend in Colorado Springs." He sighed. "But then, no doubt I'd just ruin his family too. I'm just better off alone." He whistled to his dog and walked out the door, hopped up on Comet, and galloped out of town.

* * * *

Sadie thundered into the Circle A and hauled Smokey to a stop. She jumped down and flicked his rein over the hitching post. Storming up the stairs of the bunkhouse, she knocked on the door. Cook looked up. "Do you think Hall has come to his senses?"

"Maybe." Lloyd thrust his hat on and opened the door. He smirked and eyed Sadie up and down. "Hello, little lady. What brings you here?"

Sadie scowled at his 'little lady' comment. "I need to see Robbie Gordon... Hall please."

"I'm sorry, Miss, you're too late. He's gone."

"Gone? What do you mean?"

"He's left, 'bout an hour ago, walked out without leaving a note or anything." Flynn took over as Lloyd marched out to take his shift.

Sadie screwed up her face. "Why? Did he say why he left?"

"Just mumbled something about ruining families and being better off alone."

Sadie was surprised at how disappointed she was. Her heart lurched and she fought the urge to break down in tears. "Oh no. It's all my fault. Please, you have to help me find him."

Cook shrugged. "Miss, we don't know where he is. He could be in any direction."

"Please, help me. We have to find him. For my aunt's sake." Sadie's lip trembled.

"You might try the boss. We can't leave without his say-so anyhow," Flynn offered. It had never occurred to Sadie to be worried about being alone with all the cowboys. She was much too upset. She'd been up late praying and seeking God and asking for forgiveness. She still didn't like Robbie, not one bit, but he didn't deserve to miss out on a family because of her, and she wanted to make it up to her aunt.

"Oh no, I have to find him." Sadie hurried out the door, hung her head, and determined she would search the entire territory to find him, even if she had to go alone. She leaped up on Smokey, whispered a prayer for guidance, and galloped toward the western path out of town.

*　*　*　*

"Jack," Beth called loudly. Jack's head flicked up. He could hear the distress in her voice. He dropped the saddle he was repairing and hurried out. Beth had tears rolling down her cheeks.

"What is it?" He put an arm out to her.

"Sadie is missing."

Jack frowned. "What do you mean?"

"She left for the ranch at nine this morning. It's past one and she hasn't returned. Do you think something's happened to her? I told her not to go alone. What if those cowboys have hurt her?"

"Don't go jumping to conclusions. I'll go out there and find her. Don't you worry, Darling. I'll find her." He embraced Beth and then wiped her tears. "Why don't you go and spend time with Annabelle? I'll find her, I promise."

"Yes, Annie can pray with me."

Jack kissed her. "I love you. And I will find her, have faith."

"I know."

*　*　*　*

"Where did she go?" Jack appealed to the cowboys.

Flynn shrugged. "Sorry, Sir, she just galloped out of here. I suspect she's trying to find Hall."

Jack shook his head. "Thank you."

"You need help looking?"

"Yeah, I might do."

"We'll get the boss and round up some people to help search."

"Meet me outside the mercantile in half an hour."

Flynn nodded to Jack and they ran to do his bidding.

Ten men assembled and split into groups of two to try every trail out of town.

*　*　*　*

Robbie pulled Comet to a stop at a river. He jumped down and let the horse drink. Ozzie was glad for the break too and thrust his own nose in the cool water. Robbie threw himself down under a tree and leaned back against it. "I wish I'd thought to bring myself some food," he murmured. "I'll have to find a rabbit I suppose."

Comet grazed nearby.

Robbie sighed and leaned his head back against the tree. He closed his eyes and let out a single sob. He reached into his knapsack and pulled out his father's pocket watch. He turned it over in his hand and flicked it open. He ran his fingers across the inscription and snapped it shut. He lifted his knees, wrapped his arms around them, and laid his head down.

"I finally found a family, a job I loved, a place I could belong. I should've known better than to let myself dream of such a life." Ozzie whimpered and walked over to lean against Robbie. The man lifted a hand to the dog, and he curled up and went to sleep at Robbie's feet.

"Oz." Robbie rubbed his dog's head. "It's just you and me and Comet now." He swallowed. "We'll be okay. We've been on our own for years. We'll make it." He looked up at the path before him. "I wish I knew where we were. We gotta get some food soon." He sighed and pulled out the New Testament from his pocket. He opened it and stared at the page. "God, why'd you bring me here, let me find family after all these years, only to rip it all away from me?"

He snapped the book shut and thrust it back into his pocket. He put his head in his hands again and let the tears come. "All I ever wanted was a family, God. It's all I ever wanted. How could You be so cruel as to dangle that carrot and then take it away again." He swallowed, sat up, and took a deep breath. He sucked back the emotion determinedly. "Well, I don't need God. He's never done anything for me. Only person I need to survive is me. I've done fine up till now. So, I don't get a family. That's just fine. If you don't love anyone, you can't get hurt." He took another deep breath, shoved his hat on his head, and stood up. He climbed up on Comet, whistled to Ozzie, and headed up the path.

He fixed his eyes on the trail before him and nudged Comet into a fast walk. He wasn't in a hurry; he had nowhere to go, so he ambled along.

*   *   *   *

"It's no good. We aren't gonna find anyone in the dark, Nelson." Turner shook his head. "We ought to turn back."

"We can't turn back. I have to find her. Please, we've got a little more light. We can sleep out here and start again in the morning. She can't have got too far. She only had a few hours head start."

Samuel Turner shrugged. "We don't know she came this way?"

"We saw a fresh deposit remember? She has to be up here…" He paused as they heard the crackle of twigs, and smelled the smoke. "Up here." Jack took off at a gallop toward the smoke.

"Wait, it could be anyone." Turner followed a little more cautiously.

Jack galloped around the corner and gasped.

Ozzie pricked up his ears and began to whine. Robbie stood up and prepared to reach for his pistol. It wasn't loaded, but no one else knew that. He was surprised to see Jack speed around the corner. He frowned and sat back down at his fire.

Jack jumped off his horse and ran over with a face full of panic. "Robbie."

"What do you want?"

"You, hopefully."

"Why?" Robbie asked as Turner joined them.

"Hall, ahhh, Gordon, I'm glad we found you."

"If you've come to take back the horse, he's just over there." Robbie gestured to the west; where the horse was grazing nearby.

Turner and Jack sat down opposite him. "I haven't come for the horse. I've come for you."

"I'm sorry I just ran out like that. I needed to get away."

"Why?" Jack asked.

"You know why. I destroyed your family, at least for Sadie." He gulped; his throat tightened. "I just found a place that was starting to feel like home. It was too good to be true. I'm destined to be alone, I guess." He shrugged. "Just my lot in life. It's okay. I'm used to it." But the tremor in his voice let them know he wasn't okay.

"Won't you come back, Robbie? It would mean the world to Beth."

"But what about Sadie? I know she hates me. If I'm not around, she'll have no reason to be upset. I wouldn't want to come between a family."

"She's missing."

"What?" Jack's words had caused an unexpected flutter in Robbie's heart. "What do you mean?"

Jack took a deep breath. "She rode out to the ranch this morning to find you, to apologize and ask you to come back. She had just been jealous and worried you'd take her Aunt Beth from her."

Robbie closed his eyes, surprised at the lurch in his heart. "Why would she apologize? She did nothing wrong. It's me that got in the way. I didn't mean to. I didn't know I even had an aunt. I didn't even know who I was. I'm grateful to Mrs. Nelson for telling me who I am, but I can't go back. I doubt Mrs. Nelson would want me back after all the turmoil I've brought with me." He closed his eyes. "I should never have come here."

"Robbie." Jack's voice was stern. "That's nonsense. Beth loves you and wants you to come home, Sadie is just hot-headed sometimes, but she has a heart of gold. She's quick to make amends. That's why she's trying to find you. But now she's missing. She left around ten a.m. trying to find you. We've got riders out, but she could be anywhere." His voice faltered.

Turner took over. "We could use your help to find her. Thought maybe your dog could help?"

"Alright, I'll help find her, and then I'll be out of your way."

"Why?" both men asked at the same time.

"I've let you both down."

"How's that?" Jack asked.

Robbie gestured to Jack. "I ruined your family, and Sadie is missing because of me." He pointed to Turner. "And I walked out on you without saying goodbye."

Turner nodded. "That's true, but I can understand why. I'm willing to overlook that, and I'd love to have you back. You're a good man Ha...Gordon. I'd be sorry to see you go."

"You'd take me back?" Robbie lifted his brows.

"Yes. But first, will you help us find the girl?"

"Of course. Do you have something with her scent on it? For Ozzie?"

Jack pulled out his handkerchief, the one he'd given Sadie to wipe her tears. "This might do. Although it's just as likely it'll have my scent."

"It might work. Better than nothing." Robbie held the handkerchief to the dog's nose. He sniffed it and leaped up and began sniffing around. He hurried over and sniffed at Jack, barking twice like he'd found his target, looking confused as to why he'd been asked to track a person sitting right there.

"It's no good. It doesn't have enough of her scent." Robbie shrugged. He felt defeated, broken. He'd made a mess of the whole situation. *Shoulda just kept roaming. Should never've come to Dusty Ridge.*

"We have to go back to town anyway. We know she's not on this trail; she would've found you." Jack shrugged.

"Let's head back. We have a little light left." Turner examined the sky.

Robbie nodded, extinguished his fire, and climbed up on Comet. Soon the three men and the dog were galloping back to town.

Twilight was approaching as they entered town. "It'll be dark soon. We'll have to go out at first light." Turner offered.

Edwards came running out of the saloon. "Any sign?"

"No. You?" Turner shook his head.

"No. The others have been back several hours. Just waiting in the saloon as per your instruction." He turned to the man who leaped off his horse. "Hall?"

"Yeah."

"You've caused a right ruckus." Edwards scowled as the men led their horses to the livery.

"Don't, Edwards. He made a mistake. I understand. We need to concentrate our efforts on the girl."

Edwards nodded to his boss. "I'll take care of the horses, Sir."

"You two come home with me. We got spare rooms. We'll leave at first light," Jack offered. "Beth will be beside herself with worry."

"I gotta go back to my family. Edith'll be worried."

Jack nodded. "Thank you, I understand, Turner. We've got it from here. With the dog, we'll find her."

"Okay, come for me if you need me. I hope you find her. We'll be praying."

"I appreciate that." Remaining stoic was how Jack was managing to not fall apart.

"Gordon, when all this is over, you come out to the ranch and we'll talk." Turner nodded to him.

"It might be better if I just leave town, Sir. I'm sure my aunt will understand." Robbie shoved his hands in his pockets.

"That's up to you. But I'll be sorry to lose you."

"But I will return your horse."

Turner gripped his shoulder. "It's yours, Robbie. You keep it."

"Thank you. I'm sorry for all this."

Turner nodded, jumped on his horse, and galloped away.

* * * *

Beth was hysterical. "Where is she? Oh, Sadie, where is she?" she cried over and over. Jack held her and tried to console her.

"I'll find her, Beth. We've got the dog now. We'll find her."

"No, please don't leave me. I can't lose you as well."

"I'll go, Ozzie and me. We'll find her and bring her back," Robbie offered.

"I'll come with you, Robbie," Jack determined.

"No, Aunt Beth needs you. This is my mess. I'll find her."

"Are you sure?"

"Yeah, I'm better off on my own. I can move faster that way. I'm used to being out in the wilderness. I'll find her, I promise."

A howling wind rattled the windows. "Be careful. I fear a storm is coming; and you've only got a limited amount of light left."

"Rest assured, I'll find her. I will bring her back. I will make this up to you." Robbie sniffed back a tear. "I'm sorry, Aunt Beth."

Beth stepped out of Jack's arms. "It's not your fault, Robbie. If anything, it's mine. Please find her, I can't bear to lose her. And be safe, now that I've found you, I don't want to lose you either." She embraced him.

"Thank you. I'll find her." Robbie thrust his hat on his head and left his sobbing aunt in the arms of Jack. He ran out the door into the twilight, thankful for the bright moon, and thrust Sadie's scarf under the nose of the dog. Ozzie began sniffing around, running back and forth with his nose to the ground. Hurrying up the western path, he barked and took off down the road.

Robbie sped off after the dog.

Nine

"Smokey. I think we're lost." Sadie frowned and shivered. The wind was coming up. She'd given up the search after three hours. She had no idea how to find a wayward cowboy. "I should've got some help." She wandered down another path, hoping it was the one that she'd come on, but they all looked the same, and she'd been galloping and didn't take in any scenery. She remembered passing a sign saying, 'Eagle Springs 5 miles,' but she couldn't find it again.

Sadie shivered and looked up the path. "Let's face it, Smokey. We're lost." Her lips trembled. "What are we going to do?"

Smokey snorted. The wind came up and it began to rain lightly. "Oh no, Smokey, we need to find shelter." She hastened the horse. A massive clap of thunder rolled overhead, causing Smokey to rear and bolt. Sadie tried to hold onto the panicked horse, but Smokey swerved, and Sadie fell, to the ground, striking her wrist on a rock and hitting her head on the hard ground. The last thing she remembered was an excruciating pain in her wrist before everything went dark.

* * * *

"God, I don't know if You are there, and I don't know if You'll even listen to me. Sadie doesn't deserve this. None of this is her fault. She's completely innocent. Please help me find her, quickly. I know I don't deserve Your favor, but she does. Please help."

They came to a fork in the road. Ozzie sniffed at the ground and headed up the left fork. Just as he did so, it began to rain. "Oh no." Robbie pulled his coat around his shoulders. "Oh no," he repeated. Ozzie came to a stop. The rain had washed out the scent. "Oh no." He grimaced as a massive clap of thunder rolled across the sky and Comet reared on his hind legs. Robbie held on and spoke soothingly to the horse. He pulled him in and managed to stop the horse from bolting, although his ears and eyes remained alert. "The last thing we need is a storm. I hope she's found shelter." Robbie pulled his hat down over his ears and kept following the left path.

Ozzie barked, and a saddled horse came running past them, reigns dangling. "Oh." Robbie turned and chased the horse down. More thunderclaps spooked the horse further. He was able to keep Comet from bolting, but Smokey led him on quite a chase, spooking and rearing in panic at each clap of thunder. The rain increased and he could hardly see.

Ozzie followed, barking loudly. "Shuddup, Oz." He was adding to the horse's terror. At last, with a final burst of speed, he rode alongside Smokey. Holding Comet's rein with one hand, he got as close as he could and leaned down as far as he dared to reach a rein.

He got a finger to it and Smokey gained speed, bolting again. Robbie sighed and reached for the rope on his saddle. He was new to roping and hadn't mastered a lariat yet, but he galloped with all his might; the road was mud, and the low light made the going harder. At last, he caught up with Smokey again. Gripping Comet with one hand, he threw the rope and missed. He pulled it back and threw it again, managing to get a wide loop around the horse's neck. It wouldn't pull tight like a lariat, but he pulled Smokey closer and bent down to grab her rein.

He pulled Comet to a halt and Smokey slowed at last. Another clap of thunder and a massive streak of lightning lit the sky up. Robbie gripped Smokey's rein as tight as he could as she tried to bolt again.

At last, she calmed and he tied his rope around her halter and, leading her, hurried back the way he'd come. At least he hoped it was the way he'd come. He grimaced, he'd backtracked miles and detoured several times, trying to catch the wayward horse. It was too small to be a man's horse, so he guessed it must have been Sadie's. She had to be close by and probably had fallen off. He had to find her.

Holding both horses tightly, through more thunderclaps, and increasingly heavy rain, he kept moving. While chasing the horse, he'd noticed a small cabin. It had probably belonged to a trapper or lumberjack at one time. If he could find that again, he'd be able to take her there. "If I can find her. Please, God," he yelled into the driving rain. Just then, Ozzie barked and hurried down a path. A clap of thunder startled the horses, but Robbie held on and followed the dog.

A flash of lightning lit up the sky and he gasped and hauled the horses to a stop, narrowly missing trampling a body on the road. He leaped off the horse, praying there'd be no more lightning till he could get her to the cabin. "Please let her be alive." He shuddered as he knelt. *Aunt Beth would never forgive me if Sadie died.* He touched her neck and felt a pulse. "Thank the Lord." But it was weak, and her skin was icy cold. He turned her over and noticed the wound on her head. "Oh no." He scooped her up in his arms, and hoisted her onto his horse. He held her there with one hand and leaped up behind her. He put an arm around her. "Now, to find that cabin. God, guide me." He frowned and decided to head north, hoping it was that way. Water ran down his neck and he shivered.

Sadie groaned and he pulled her tightly toward himself, hoping to pass some of his body warmth onto her, she was absolutely sodden. He could barely see more than a foot in front of him, the driving rain swirled, and the sky rumbled, threatening more thunder.

Robbie gripped Sadie tightly. "God," he called as loudly as he could into the storm. "Where are you?" Tears coursed down his cheeks, mingling with the rainwater on his face. "Please save her. I'll give my life in her place, but please save her, for Aunt Beth's sake. I'll trade places. Take me, not her," he pleaded. "I need the cabin, God. Please. I need the cabin." He looked up and peered into the darkness. Ozzie ran forward, veered off the path and began to bark. It was the cabin. Ozzie scratched and whined at the door.

"Thank you, God." The cabin was abandoned. It had a small, rather dilapidated shed next to it. He sighed with relief, there was a place for the horses. He jumped down from the horse holding Sadie in place, then reached up and lifted her down. Praying the horses would stay put, he ran to the cabin door and thrust his foot at the lock. It broke open with a spray of dust. Robbie staggered in and looked around. It was dark, but he could just make out a bed in the corner. He hurried over, thrust the wet shawl off her and placed her on the bed. She really needed to be out of the wet clothes but how? Throwing a blanket over her, he hurried outside. Yanking both horses, he hauled them into the small shed, beyond grateful to find a stack of old straw inside.

"Sorry, it's not much, but it'll have to do." He hoisted the saddles off the horses, threw them over a rail, and pulled the door shut behind them, hoping the shed would withstand the storm.

"Come on, Oz," he called to the dog and ran inside. He closed the door tightly and looked around. Thrusting his hand inside his very wet knapsack, he fished around. The water had made its way inside, but he prayed his matches would be dry. He struck one and sighed with relief as it lit. He held it up and looked around. There was a lantern on the wall. He snatched at it and lit the wick, relieved as the light illuminated the cabin.

The wind and rain pounded at the small cabin and the windows and door rattled. He held up the lantern and looked around. The cabin was small but well-equipped. A small kitchen with a larder, a fireplace, two armchairs and a settee, a table, two chairs, and the bed. It looked to have been abandoned for some time. A layer of dust coated the house. A pile of wood was stacked beside the fireplace.

Robbie heard Sadie groan. He had to get her warm. He knew little about caring for a sick person, but Mrs. Bonnie had always insisted they stay warm when they were sick. First, he needed to get the chill off the air. He hastened to light a fire in the brick fireplace. He had it going quickly. It smoked a lot. but the warmth slowly began to penetrate the air.

"Now to get her warm." He grimaced. *I need to get her wet things off her, but should I? Can I?* Robbie groaned *I don't want to do anything inappropriate, but what if it costs her life?*

With a sigh, Robbie closed his eyes tightly and walked over to her. "Forgive me." Sitting her up he undid the buttons on her dress. Carefully lifting it over her head, he grimaced. It was putting her in a compromising position, but the less wet clothing she had on, the better. Besides, he had no intention of doing anything inappropriate. He just wanted to get her warm. Picking up the dry blanket from the end of the bed, he wrapped her in it, laid her down and walked over to the fire. He pushed one armchair away, and coughed as he stirred up the dust.

Pulling the small settee as close to the fire as he dared, Robbie carried Sadie across and lay her on it. He touched her face. Her cheeks were still icy, but she would warm soon.

He was saturated, and trembling with the cold, but he didn't care. His first priority was to get her warm. Only then would he consider himself.

Content he'd done all he could for now, he snatched her discarded dress and hung it over the armchair to dry by the fire.

He shivered again. Ozzie crowded as close to the fire as he could get, and shook the water off himself, causing the fire to steam. The dog put his head on his paws and curled up, trying to get warm.

Robbie shivered again. Now that he'd done all he could for Sadie, he had to get himself dry. He yanked his clothes from his bag; they were damp but better than what he currently had on. He changed quickly and hung his wet clothes before the fire.

He threw another dry blanket around himself and sat before the fire in the armchair. For almost an hour, he sat and shivered, keeping one eye on Sadie. The storm continued to shake the windows. Every thunderclap and lightning strike brought agitated whinnies from the horses. "God, please protect the horses. I'm gonna need them to get us back to town." The storm looked to be set in and he grimaced. "Sorry, Aunt Beth."

He'd just found this family, and now he faced bringing his aunt the sad news that Sadie had died. He pleaded with God over and over in the wee small hours of the morning. "I'll give my life, God, just save her. I beg of you."

Ten

Beth sat staring into the flames. She had no more tears. Her eyes were dark from weeping and her face pale. Jack had done everything he could to reassure her, but with the storm raging outside, she was certain Sadie and Robbie were never coming back.

Jack prayed without ceasing. Several times he'd determined to go out and find them, but that would just leave Beth all alone. If the worst was to happen, he needed to be there for Beth. He couldn't have her lose him too.

He paced back and forth, praying. He couldn't get Beth to eat or drink or speak. She just stared at the fire and whimpered occasionally. At close to midnight, he picked her up and carried her to their bedroom, removed her shoes, and placed her in bed. He climbed in next to her and wrapped his arms around her to comfort her with his body, all the while continuing to pray without ceasing.

*   *   *   *

Warm at last, Robbie stood, and turned all the clothing around to dry on the other side. The room was pungent; the smell of dust, wet dog, steaming clothing, and something he couldn't place, made for an unpleasant environment, but at least they were dry. The little cabin, rough as it was, was weather tight and he was grateful for that.

He checked on Sadie. Her cheeks were warm, and he was sure she would wake up soon. He loosened the blanket a little and pushed the settee a little further from the flames. The room was warm now.

Sadie groaned and he grimaced. "Please, God. Help me." His stomach started to growl. Sadie would soon need to eat. He hurried to the little kitchen and took stock of what he had. Lifting the lantern, he opened the larder. Dust flew in his face, he coughed and wiped his eyes. He peered inside. There was flour, sugar, and a few other staples. Several jars of preserves, peaches, and what looked to be apples. On the next shelf were plates and cups and a jar with cutlery standing up in it.

The bottom shelf had spices and more preserves: carrots, beans, and a few unmarked, unopened tins.

Robbie walked toward the bed to continue his inventory of the cabin. Opening a trunk, he found clothing, even a woman's dress, a hairbrush, a few books, and two pairs of men's trousers and a shirt.

There was a shelf by the bed that had a single faded photograph, of a young couple. A shotgun hung above the fireplace, and he found bullets on another shelf.

A clap of lightning illuminated the room for a moment, and he grimaced as the horses whinnied again. The storm didn't look to be letting up anytime soon.

He finished his tour of the cabin, noticing a coat rack with two coats, a man's and a smaller one Robbie presumed was a woman's, two pairs of boots, a large and small pair, and two hats.

"A couple must have lived here at one point." It did look like a woman had been there. There was a colorful, crazy quilt on the bed, homemade rugs on the floor, and fluffy curtains in the window. Whoever had lived there had done their utmost with the little they had.

Sadie groaned and Robbie scooped her up, lest she fall off the settee. He unwrapped her from the blanket, pulled down the bed-clothes, and placed her in, pulling the blankets up to her neck.

She sweated profusely as fever took her. "Oh no." He closed his eyes and bit his lips for a moment. There was one more cupboard, which he sincerely hoped might hold something that was medicinal.

He hurried to open it, only to find it contained sheets, towels, and little else. He sighed and pumped some water into a steel basin and hung it over the fire to warm. He grabbed a towel from the cupboard, sliced it in half with his knife, and pumped water over it. He ran to Sadie and placed the cool cloth on her forehead.

Robbie creased his brow. Did you sweat out a fever or try to cool the person down? And then there was her head injury. There was a large bruise above her left eye.

The cold cloth calmed her a little, and Robbie pulled a dining chair close to the bed and flopped into it to watch her.

Robbie put his hands over his face and leaned his elbows on his knees. *Why did I ever come to this town? All of this is my fault. I never should've accepted the invitation to lunch after church. I should've walked away. I was beginning to hope for a happily ever after in this town, but all I've done is bring disaster. If I manage to get Sadie through this, I'll leave and never come back. I'll go back to roaming. If I'm alone, I can't cause heartache for anyone else. Maybe this is why I don't have a family. It's too painful.*

He looked up at Sadie. His heart ached for her. He couldn't shake the hurt, the worry, and the guilt. He broke down in sobs pleading with God to help her.

Sadie groaned again, and Robbie snapped out of his funk. "God, save her. Take me instead. Please save her," he said for the umpteenth time.

Robbie tended to her the best he could all night. He didn't sleep; he wouldn't. He couldn't. He had to save her. Daylight came, and still, the fever raged, and so did the storm.

* * * *

Beth didn't get out of bed for the entirety of the next day. The livery remained closed while Jack watched out for Beth. He held her, prayed with her, and tried to get her to eat, but she was beside herself.

Jack brought a bowl of soup, and Beth sat up in bed staring into space. "Beth. You must have faith. God is with us, my darling, and He is with Sadie and Robbie, no matter what happens. I'll bet he's found her by now, and they're just waiting out the storm, sheltered somewhere. They'll be home when it stops." He desperately tried to reassure her.

She raised sad eyes to him. "I hope so."

"Darling." Jack kissed his wife. "No matter what happens, you have me, and you have the Lord. We can carry on in the face of any trial in our life because of the Lord. Will you trust Him?"

Beth nodded. "Will you pray with me?" They were the first words she'd spoken in two days.

"Absolutely." He put the soup aside, sat up on the bed with his wife, and petitioned the Lord for strength and courage. He committed both young people into God's hands.

"Remember, Darling, there are no safer hands than God's."

"Thank you for reminding me. I feel His peace, His arms around me. I won't worry and fret any longer. I'll trust God with them."

"That's my girl." Jack kissed her forehead. "Will you come and have supper with me?"

"Certainly."

He helped her out of bed and to the kitchen. Beth's newfound resolve helped her carry on, with the Lord's strength. Still, she prayed without ceasing, and still, the storm raged.

*　*　*　*

"Whaaa... Whhaaa..." Sadie began to moan. Her fever had broken a few hours earlier.

Robbie placed a cold cloth on her head. "It's okay, Sadie. It's okay. You're safe." *Thank the Lord.*

She opened her eyes at last and looked around. "Where am I?"

"It's okay; you're safe, Sadie. I found you. You fell off your horse and hurt yourself. I brought you here to shelter from the storm, and you've had a fever." He touched her forehead. "It broke a few hours ago."

"How long?" Her voice was barely a whisper.

"Three days. You can see the storm is still raging. As soon as it stops, and you're well enough, I'll get you home. I imagine Aunt Beth is beside herself."

Sadie tried to lift her arm and groaned loudly.

"Your wrist?"

"Yes."

He gently touched it, and she flinched and cried out.

He grimaced. "Oh no. I suspect it's broken. I'll find something to splint it, just in case."

She nodded.

"Here, I'll help you sit up."

She nodded again. He pulled down the covers and she gasped. "You undressed me?"

"I had to get you out of the wet dress." He screwed up his face.

She grasped the blankets in her good hand and pulled them up to her neck. "You undressed me?" She shuddered.

Robbie stood to fetch a sheet from the cupboard and two wooden spoons. He broke the heads off the spoons and began tearing the sheet into strips as he returned to his chair. He looked at Sadie, contrition all over his face. "I'm sorry if I overstepped the bounds. It seems I've been doing a lot of that lately. You were soaked to the skin, I had to get at least one layer of clothing off you, to warm you up. Your dress is over there by the fire." He gestured to her. "I promise you; I didn't look. I've been honorable, and I have no intention of hurting you or being inappropriate."

Sadie nodded, and conversations with her uncle and the doctor floated into her mind. "I understand. You did what you had to. Cotton underthings would certainly dry faster without a wet dress clinging to them. But I can't stay in my undergarments. I need to get dressed."

"Let me splint your wrist first, and then I'll have to help you. You can't do anything with that hand. I'm sorry, I didn't know it was broken until you woke up."

She smiled at him. He gently lifted her arm and she groaned loudly. He laid the makeshift bandage underneath and the two wooden spoon handles on either side, to hold the wrist stiffly in place. As gently as he could, he wound the strip of cotton around and around until her wrist and hand were held firm. He then tore a square from the sheet and laid it aside.

"Let me help you sit up, and then I'll get your dress."

Sadie nodded, seething internally that she was beholden to him yet again. But there was something strangely nice about his gentle manner. *Perhaps he isn't as awful as I thought. Perhaps, I misjudged him. After all, he's been here three days looking after me.* "Thank you," she whispered.

Robbie smiled. "You're most welcome, Miss Nelson. I'm glad you're letting me help you."

At last, he had her sitting up and hurried to get her dress. With her one good arm, Sadie helped to get it over her head. Robbie deftly did up the buttons at the back. Reaching for the square of cotton, he folded it into a triangle, and created a sling for her arm, tying it around her neck.

Just as he finished, an enormous clap of thunder and a bolt of lightning lit up the sky. The horses whinnied in fright, and they heard an almighty crash as a tree fell nearby. The entire cabin shook, and dust rained down on them.

"Wow." Sadie's eyes were wide. "This is some storm."

"Yeah. It hasn't let up for three days."

She nodded and looked around. Her arm was in agony, and she had a massive headache, but she tried to ignore it. Her mind was still woozy, and she felt very weak.

Robbie sat back down on the chair next to her, and relief shone from his eyes. "I'm glad you're well. I prayed and prayed that God would make you well."

Sadie tipped her head to the side.

"Why?"

"What do you mean?"

"Why do you care? I was awful to you."

"I wasn't about to let you die out there. Aunt Beth would never forgive me. I promised I'd find you and bring you home, and I plan to do that. Then I'll leave, and your life can go back to how it was."

"Why?"

"Because I've ruined everything. Interfered with your family."

"No, you didn't; I did." She looked contrite. "I'm sorry."

"Why are you sorry? I'm the one who pushed my way in. I'm afraid I don't know how to be in a family, and I sure never meant to hurt any of you." He shrugged, stood up, and walked to the kitchen to put coffee on and fetch Sadie some food. "I guess that's why I'm better off alone."

"Well, that's nonsense." Sadie screwed up her face at him.

Robbie shook his head and brought over two cups of coffee, and a bowl of stewed apple with a spoon. He laid them on the trunk beside the bed and resumed his seat. Offering her a cup, he took the other. Both slurped at their coffee in silence.

Sadie lowered her cup and looked up at him. "For what's it worth, I'm sorry."

Robbie raised his brows.

"For being so awful to you. Uncle Jack and Dr. Chapman both told me you were just being kind. I'm afraid my emotions get the better of me sometimes..." She grimaced and sighed. "God's got a lot of work to do on me, I'm afraid."

Robbie nodded. "Me too."

"Are you a Christian, Robbie?"

He lifted his eyes to meet hers. "Yeah. A somewhat lapsed one, if I'm honest." Robbie shrugged and scratched his chin. "I kinda feel sometimes like God has forgotten about me."

"That's nonsense," Sadie scolded him and sipped at her coffee. "Just because things don't go your way, it doesn't mean God isn't looking out for you. We have to count our blessings in life. Not dwell on the hardships." Her lip trembled.

"Yeah. I guess you're right. I was just starting to feel like I finally found a home, a place to belong." He sighed and hung his head. "But I went and ruined it. So, Ozzie and I will get you home, then we'll leave town."

Sadie put her coffee down and put a hand out to him. Something about his vulnerability endeared him to her. She remembered the doctor's words about how wonderful it was to be dependent on others and have them depend on you. She'd tried to push others away, and here was Robbie, longing for someone to depend on, but he'd never had that chance. Now that he did, she wasn't about to take it from him. She squeezed his arm. "You have."

He looked up at her and frowned. "I have what?"

"Found your place to belong. In Dusty Ridge, with us."

Robbie leaned forward, draped his arms over his knees, and stared at his boots. "But you've made it clear you don't want me in the family."

Sadie sighed and leaned her head back against the wall. "I'm sorry. I didn't stop to think how it must be for you and for Aunt Beth, to have you come back from the dead like that after all these years. I would give anything to see one of my family again after all this time, and if I did, I'd wrap my arms around them and never ever let them go. So, I understand. Will you forgive my impetuousness?"

Robbie looked up and gave her a sideways smile. "I reckon so. If you'll forgive my intrusion into your family."

"No."

He frowned.

"Because there is nothing to forgive. You've done nothing wrong."

He shrugged. "Still, I think it's best I move on. I never stay in one place this long usually. It was just an impossible dream."

"Why?"

"I thought I wanted a home and a family. But it's obvious I don't know how to do that, or what it means to be family."

"Love. That's all it is. You have to love each other to the best of your ability. That's all family is. It's got nothing to do with blood. I don't have blood in common with either Aunt Beth or Uncle Jack, but I couldn't love them more if they were my own parents."

"I thought he was your uncle?"

"Yes, my father's brother."

Robbie furrowed his brow; she wasn't making sense.

Sadie grinned. "They were both adopted from different families, but that didn't matter. They were just brothers."

He nodded. "I see. Do you mind me asking how you came to be with them?"

He lifted the bowl and held it out to her so she could scoop the apple up and eat. She took three mouthfuls then laid the spoon down. "My parents and sister were killed in the war when the soldiers came. I was a year old, and my mother hid me in her armoire. Later when Uncle Jack and Aunt Beth heard what had happened, they came to the house looking for me. By some miracle, the soldiers hadn't burned the house. They'd burned everything else. Anyhow Uncle Jack heard me screaming. I'd been in there two days."

"Brave girl."

"Uncle Jack tells me it's why God gave me so much stubbornness. I refused to give up even then."

Both raised their faces to look out the window. The rain had stopped.

"Praise God." Robbie swiped at his forehead. "How are you feeling?"

"Weak. I have a massive headache, and my wrist is on fire."

"I bet; your body has worked hard to fight the fever. You get some sleep, and in the morning, I'll get us home."

"Thank you."

"You don't have to thank me, Sadie." He stood and helped her lie down in the bed, pulling the blankets up around her chin. "You sleep. I'll be here by the fire."

"When was the last time you slept?" She noticed the exhaustion on his face.

He shrugged. "I haven't really, dozed a bit here and there."

"Why not?"

"I couldn't, not until I knew you were well."

Sadie gulped. The sincerity in his eyes touched her. "Well, you must sleep now. You'll be the one who's sick if you aren't careful."

"I will try, now that I know you're out of danger. Thank the Lord. I've sat here all night begging Him to save you. I asked Him to take me instead of you. To make sure you were well."

Sadie tipped her head to the side. "You said that?"

"Over and over again."

She squinted. "You'd give your life for me?"

Robbie nodded and scratched his chin. "Without question." His face and eyes confirmed his sincerity.

Sadie lay back quietly for a moment considering his words. Robbie leaned back in his chair.

"You're wrong you know."

He snapped his head up to look at her.

"You do know how to be in a family. Love is all a family is. And you know how to do that."

Robbie shrugged. "I'm not so sure. I just make it up as I go along. Try to do right by people."

"The Bible says there is no greater love than to lay down your life for a friend."

He raised his brows. "Are you saying we're friends, Miss Nelson?"

Sadie gave him a wry smile. "I'd like to be."

Robbie nodded. "I'd like that too. Get some sleep. The sun'll be up soon. I'll stay here till you're asleep, make sure the fever doesn't return."

She smiled and closed her eyes. Robbie watched until she fell asleep. He looked at her, now free from the fever. Her face had a large bruise, and her hair was a mess, but she was still very lovely. He smiled. She'd allowed herself to be vulnerable with him, and it was endearing. He admired her strength, but this new softness was intriguing.

"Too bad I have to leave. I'd have liked to have spent more time with you, Sadie Nelson. You're rather perplexing," he whispered. He stood and, on an impulse, kissed her forehead. He grimaced. *Overstepping my bounds again.*

He swallowed back the tumultuous feelings growing inside him. They were not unlike the tempest that had been raging outside. He walked over to the armchair, lifted the blanket over himself, and whistled to Ozzie. The dog leaped up onto his lap, and he put his hand on the dog's head, laid back, and fell asleep.

Eleven

Sadie woke up and blinked several times. Robbie sat by her bed again, eyes closed, murmuring to himself. She smiled. *He's praying.* He had his small New Testament open in his hands. She noticed it was upside down, and she squinted. "Morning."

He flicked open his eyes and smiled. "Morning, have a good sleep?"

"Yes. I feel a bit stronger this morning, but my wrist is sore."

"It will be for a time. Want some breakfast?"

"Soon. First, why don't you read something to me." She gestured to the book in his hands.

Robbie swallowed. "Um, what do you want me to read?"

"How about your favorite passage of scripture."

He nodded and tried to keep the flush from his cheeks. He turned a few pages and stared at the words, then quoted from memory, "The Lord is my Shepherd, I shall not want..." He paused when Sadie put her hand on his arm.

Robbie looked up at her.

Her eyes were full of compassion. "You can't read, can you?"

He hung his head. "How do you know?"

Sadie squeezed his arm and smiled. "The Bible is upside down, and you quoted a Psalm, that's not in the New Testament."

Robbie shrugged and stared at his boots.

"Why did you never learn?"

He shrugged again. "Just never picked it up beyond a few letters. Too stupid I guess."

Sadie sat up abruptly, causing her head to spin. She shook her head and put her hand out to lift his chin. She got that steely, determined look in her eye and pursed her lips at him. "You are not stupid."

He shrugged. "Figured I must be, never did pick it up. Never even went to school. Mrs. Bonnie taught us at the orphanage. My friend Timothy took to letters right away."

"Do you want to learn?" Sadie smiled at him compassionately, sensing a way she could return his kindness.

"Sure, not sure it'll do any good, though."

"Stop that. I'd be happy to teach you, to read and write."

He slumped back in the chair. "I thank you for the offer, but you'd be wasting your time. I'm fine how I am. I get by."

"Get by? Don't you want to do more than just get by? Don't you have dreams of having your own business one day or reading stories to your children?"

Robbie blushed and shrugged again. "Always thought I might own a livery one day, but I can't do the job properly if I can't even read. Children? That's an impossible dream." He shook his head and sighed loudly.

I'd like to try to change his mind about that. The thought caught Sadie off guard. She was really softening to him.

"No, it isn't. I'd be happy to teach you." She put her hand out to him. "No one would have to know, if you're embarrassed about it. Please, will you let me?"

"Sure." He shrugged. "Now, let me get you breakfast."

She nodded and shuffled back so she was against the wall. Her head still spun, and she felt weak, but determination grew in her, and the idea of someone depending on her was strangely thrilling. She was beginning to understand the doctor's words.

*　*　*　*

It was another whole day before Robbie declared Sadie strong enough to go home. He refused to let her help clean up. "We ought to go home. Come on, I'll help you up."

She smiled and put her good arm around his neck as he lifted her out of bed and put her on her feet. "Steady?"

She gripped the chair. "A little weak, but I'll be okay." She glanced at herself in the small mirror. "Oh, I look a fright." She pulled a pin out of her hair and let it tumble down her back. "What I wouldn't give for a hairbrush." She grimaced.

Something occurred to Robbie, and he grinned and hurried to the trunk. "I saw one in here when I was looking for medicine." He pulled it out and passed it to her.

She grinned and tried futilely to brush her hair. It was difficult without her other hand. Robbie watched her struggle and walked over to her. He gently touched her hand and took the brush. She lowered her hand, and her cheeks flushed as he ran the brush through her hair in long strokes. Her heart began to race just a little.

"Your hair is beautiful, Sadie." Robbie smiled at her as he finished the job. "It has just a touch of red in it." His voice was dreamy and he swallowed. He looked up at her in the mirror, his heart raced, and his cheeks warmed. "You're beautiful." He brushed her cheek gently with his knuckles, and then gasped and walked away, put the hairbrush down, and stood looking into the fire.

Sadie bit her lip and touched the spot on her cheek where he'd touched her. She turned to him.

"I'm sorry," came his quiet voice.

"For what?" She approached him.

He turned to look at her, eyes full of contrition. "Overstepping my bounds again. I really am sorry. I just got carried away in the moment. Your hair is so beautiful."

Sadie walked up to him and her cheeks reddened deeply. Lifting her eyes to his, she smiled. "Please don't be sorry. It was nice of you to say."

He swallowed. With her hair out like that and her eyes shining, he found her incredibly beautiful despite the smudges and bruises on her face. He had to fight the urge to take her in his arms and kiss her. *Robbie Gordon, are you in love with Sadie?* He had to admit he certainly was beginning to feel that way.

They looked into each other's eyes for a moment, neither saying anything. Robbie forced himself to break the gaze, lest his resolve crumbled and he kissed her. He couldn't afford to fall for her. He'd be leaving town as soon as he got her home.

*   *   *   *

"Jack, what's the matter?"

"Nothing. I'm fine." He looked up at Beth across the table.

"You were far away, and you look very pale."

"My head's a little thick, but I'll be fine."

"I hope you aren't coming down with something."

"I'm sure it's nothing. Neither of us have had much sleep, is all."

Beth's lip trembled. "It's been five days." Her voice was barely a whisper. "The storm stopped yesterday."

Jack closed his eyes as his head spun. He forced his mind to focus and gripped her hand. "They'll be fine."

"What if they never come home?"

"No despair, rem...." Jack's sentence was cut off as he broke down in a fit of coughing.

Beth leaped to her feet and ran to his side. "Jack, are you alright?"

He pulled out his handkerchief and held it to his mouth as the coughing became more severe. When at last it stopped, he pulled away the handkerchief, and there was blood on it.

"Oh no, Jack. We better get you to the doctor." *Please, Lord, don't take Jack as well. I need him. I can't lose him too.*

He stood from the chair and walked over to get his hat but fell to the floor and began convulsing and coughing up blood. "Jack. No... Jack!" Beth knelt beside him, uncertain of what to do. He stopped and groaned. "I gotta get the doc." She didn't want to leave him but had little choice. Hurrying outside, she found the Sanders boy trimming a tree in their yard. "Help, get the doctor. Jack's collapsed."

He nodded, dropped the clippers, and ran for the clinic.

*　*　*　*

Robbie entered the cabin. "The horses are ready. Come on. I'll help you up on Comet."

Sadie stood up. "I can ride myself."

"No, you can't. You're still much too weak, and how will you hold on with your arm in a sling?"

She thrust her hand on her hip and scowled at him. " 'Spose you want to hold me like I'm some damsel in distress who needs a brave knight to rescue her." Sadie's determined nature had returned.

Robbie touched her arm. "You know I don't think that about you. You're the toughest girl I know. I just want to get you back to Aunt Beth safe and sound. The easiest way is if you sit in front of me, so I can hold onto you. You won't be able to hold on to me with your broken wrist."

Sadie began to argue until previous conversations floated in her ears. *There is nothing wrong with being dependent on someone.* She was warming to the idea. Besides, the thought of his arms around her wasn't entirely unpleasant. She chuckled internally. *Sadie Nelson, are you falling for this man? A short time ago, you hated him and couldn't wait for him to leave town. Now you're determined to make him stay.* "Alright."

Robbie nodded his thanks to her for not making this any more difficult than it needed to be. His heart began to race but he stifled that thought. He was only doing what was necessary to get her home, nothing more. He was still determined to leave as soon as possible.

"Come on, Oz." He gestured to the dog, opened the door for Sadie, and they walked out. He tightly shut the door, beyond thankful to the previous owners for the little cabin that had saved their lives.

Smokey was tied with a rope to Comet's saddle. Robbie had loaded her with her saddle, and his bag. He'd taken the liberty of giving Sadie the small coat he found hanging on the wall. He didn't like to steal, but she had nothing but her shawl, and it wasn't warm outside. He wrapped it around her and lifted her up onto the horse. She clutched the rein with one hand while he climbed up behind her. He fought the flutter in his heart as he put his arms around her. Her long hair tantalizingly close to his nose. Even after all that had happened, he could still smell her lavender soap. It sent his heart racing. *No! Pull yourself together,*

Hall... ah, Gordon. You'll be leaving town soon. He took a deep breath. "Comfortable?"

Sadie's heart was pounding in her ears. Something about having Robbie's arms around her made her head spin. "Yes." She breathed out.

"Good." He took the reins. "Let's hope I can find the way home." He clucked his tongue to Comet. "Home, Oz." The dog barked twice and headed down the trail.

"Does he know the way?"

Robbie shrugged. "Better than I do. He's always had an uncanny sense of direction."

Sadie nodded and leaned back into him, groaning as her wrist bumped against her.

"Oh, is your arm hurting you?"

Sadie could hear genuine compassion in his voice. "A little, but I'm okay."

"I'll take you straight to the doc when we get home." Robbie hadn't meant to call Dusty Ridge 'home'; it had slipped out inadvertently.

Sadie caught the slip. *I'll show you that it really is your home, and we really are your family.* She bit her lip and blushed, thankful he couldn't see her face. *I wouldn't mind being your family.* She had to admit; her feelings were really changing. Robbie wasn't the aloof drifter she thought him to be. He was a kind and considerate man, and she, without meaning to, found him growing on her.

They rode in silence for a time and Sadie yawned.

"You, okay?"

"Just tired."

"I bet. You haven't really had much sleep. You can sleep while we ride. I'll make sure you don't fall."

Sadie nodded and leaned back against him.

"You might be more comfortable sitting across the saddle. Then you can lay your head on me." There was a slight quiver to his voice.

She nodded. He pulled the horse to a stop and held her by the waist. "Flick your leg over." She did so, the side with the broken wrist facing towards the horse's head. "Lie back here." He gulped as she laid her head against his chest. A tremble ran through him, and his heart skipped. It was a wonderful feeling having her lie against him. He fought the urge to wrap his arms around her and kiss her hair. He took a deep breath. "Comfortable?"

She nodded.

"Good." He spoke into her hair. He touched her shoulder briefly. "Try to sleep. We're a whole day from home as far as I can figure it."

Sadie closed her eyes, and the rolling motion of the horse lulled her to sleep. Robbie gulped. Her trust in him was overwhelming. He rode with one hand for a time, the other gently holding her. His heart began to melt. How he longed to be able to give his heart to such a woman. To truly know what it is to belong to a family, to be dependent on her and have her depend on him. He'd noticed a real softening in her, and it thrilled him when she let him help her, when she was vulnerable like she was in his arms. He leaned forward and kissed her hair. He sat back and gasped, "Overstepping your bounds again." He put both hands back on the rein and did his utmost to concentrate on the path ahead of them.

*   *   *   *

Beth sat beside Jack's bed in the clinic. The large open room they called 'the ward' was next to the main examination room. It had four beds, each divided by small nib walls the doctor had put between them to afford each patient some semblance of privacy, although everything could be heard through them. Beth gripped her husband's hand and sobbed. The doctor had given Jack something to help him sleep. He'd gone to check on another patient, a spinster in her fifties, Miss Irene Neville, who was in the next cubicle recovering after having had her spleen removed.

The doctor told Beth it was likely Jack had a nasty ulcer, but he couldn't rule out something worse, like a tumor. It would take more testing, and he needed to do some reading in the latest journals to make sure he got the diagnosis correct.

In the meantime, Jack was stable and sleeping, and Beth had calmed. She clung desperately to her faith, and there found the courage to carry on.

Twelve

"Sadie," Robbie spoke to her. "Sadie." He shook her gently. "Wake up. We're almost home."

She sat up and looked around. "How long was I asleep?"

"Several hours. It's nearly dusk; we'll be home in a few moments. Dusty Ridge is just around the corner."

"Thank you, Robbie." She looked up at him. "You saved my life."

"My pleasure." He caught her eye for a moment and then hastily looked away. The look in her eye was too much. His resolve was already crumbling. *I'd love to feel how soft her lips are.* He took a deep breath and squashed down those feelings. "I'll drop you at the infirmary; then I'll go by the house and tell Aunt Beth you're here."

"And then?"

"I'll make sure you're home, safe and sound; bring Aunt Beth to you, and then I'll leave town."

"You still mean to leave?" She was unable to keep the tremble from her voice.

Robbie shrugged. "Nothing to stay for."

"There's family?"

"It's a nice dream, Sadie, but I'm not cut out for staying put. I've been roaming for years, and I told you, I don't know how to have a family."

"I wish you'd stay."

"I wish I could too. If ever there was a place that could've been my home, it would be here." He sighed loudly. "But if it won't work out here, I can't see it ever happening." He sighed and resigned himself to a life of roaming.

"I wanted to teach you to read and write."

He shrugged again. "I'll be fine. I've survived this long without doing it."

"What about your dream?"

"What dream?"

"You told me you wanted to run a livery one day."

"I want a great many things I can't have." He sighed loudly.

Sadie closed her eyes. *Why can't he see that everything he wants is just at arm's length, and all he has to do is reach out and take it? Oh Lord, please minister to his heart. Show him that he is needed, loved, and wanted here. That this can be his home. I'd sure like to give him a home.* She admitted in her heart and bit her lip.

"We're here." They walked up the main street.

A gasp came from the direction of the café, and a woman pointed. "Look."

The sheriff leaned against the awning post drinking his coffee. He put the cup down and walked towards the approaching horse. "Robbie, Sadie, we've been looking for you. Glad to know you're okay."

"We holed up in a cabin to wait out the storm. Sadie had a fever, and she has a broken wrist." Robbie pulled up and Sadie sat up. "I couldn't leave until she was strong enough."

"Oh!" The sheriff approached and reached up for Sadie. "I'm glad you're well again, Miss Nelson." He made sure she was steady on her feet and turned back to his coffee cup.

"Sadie, go to the infirmary and I'll see to the horses."

"I wish you wouldn't go." Sadie put a hand on Robbie's leg.

"Ahhh, Robbie, Jack is in the infirmary," the sheriff offered.

"What?" Sadie's hand flew to her mouth.

Robbie frowned and jumped down off his horse. "What do you mean?" He put a supportive hand on Sadie's back without realizing he did it.

"Got rushed in last night, coughing blood." The sheriff took Robbie's horse and hitched it.

"Oh no." Sadie's knees buckled, and she threw herself against Robbie. Not caring about the pain in her arm.

He lifted her into his arms, fearing she was going to faint. "Come on, let's go to him."

"Aunt Beth..." Sadie called as they walked in.

"Ohhhhh." Beth ran over to them as Robbie placed Sadie gently on the next bed. "Oh, my darling. Ohhh." She hugged Sadie and looked at her arm. "I'm so glad to see you're okay."

"She had a fever. We sheltered in a cabin for five nights while she recovered, and she has a broken wrist," Robbie said matter-of-factly while the doctor walked over to check on her.

Two cubicles away, Miss Neville sat up in bed drinking tea. She gasped and put her hand to her mouth. "Well, I never," she whispered.

Sadie looked up at Aunt Beth and then at Robbie. Her eyes sparkled. "He saved my life, Aunt Beth."

"Oh, Robbie." Beth threw herself in his arms. He held her while she wept. "Thank you. I'm so glad you found her and kept her safe."

"You're welcome. I promised I would."

Beth stood and kissed his cheek. "I'm so glad you're both safe. I need you both so much, especially now that Jack is sick."

The doctor inspected Sadie's arm. "You did a good job with this, Rob. And you've tended this bruise on her head."

Robbie shrugged. "Did my best with what little we had on hand. I was more worried about the fever. She's still quite weak."

"I'll check her out. Thank you, Robbie." The doctor turned to Sadie. "Let me get you a pillow and we'll sit you up." He snatched a pillow off the next bed and poked it in behind her. He frowned. "You've missed a button on your dress.

Sadie smiled. "Robbie had to help me with my dress since I couldn't do up the buttons myself." She lifted her sore arm.

All eyes swung to Robbie's. He blushed. "Nothing inappropriate happened if that's what you're thinking. I just had to get her sodden dress off her so I could warm her up. I didn't take anything else off her and I didn't look. I promise that's all and I immediately wrapped her in blankets to warm her up."

"I believe you. That was smart thinking. The less wet clothing on her, the better. You did what you had to do, and I understand." The doctor nodded at them both.

"Well, I never," Miss Neville said aloud, but no one heard her.

"You'll be fine, Miss Nelson. I'll strap this arm up and it'll heal nicely, and you'll be up and about in no time, thanks to Robbie here. He certainly saved your life, Miss Nelson." The doctor winked at her, and Sadie knew he was reminding her of their earlier conversation.

"How's Uncle Jack?"

"He's sleeping."

"Can I see him?"

"Sure."

The doctor helped her down and they walked to the next cubicle. For a reason Robbie couldn't place he followed.

The two women fell into the chairs beside Jack's bed. "Ohhhh." Sadie stroked his pale face. "Oh, Uncle Jack."

"He's going to be fine, isn't he, Doc?" Beth looked up at him.

The doctor grimaced. He didn't believe in telling lies.

"I'll leave you to it." Robbie shrugged and turned to walk away.

Sadie reached her good hand out to him. "Robbie, won't you please stay?"

He turned to look at Sadie. "Why?"

She stood and tears flooded her eyes. "I need you. I can't deal with this alone." She leaned against his chest and burst into tears.

Robbie put an arm around her and gulped. He wasn't used to people depending on him. It was both wonderful and terrifying at the same time. His feelings were all over the place, and seeing Sadie cry had made his heart ache. "Alright, I'll stay till Uncle Jack is up and about." He rubbed her back and leaned his head on hers.

"Thank you." She nodded against his chest.

He released her and she resumed her seat. Robbie stood behind her and placed his hand on her shoulder.

"What is it, Doctor?" Beth frowned.

Robbie put a hand on Beth's shoulder too and squatted down behind them.

"I've been reading up on his symptoms." The look on the doctor's face made Beth gasp, she gripped Sadie's hand and both women looked to the doctor.

"I'm sorry to tell you, I believe he does have a tumor, based on the pain and the blood, and the tests I could manage to run in this clinic."

Both women sniffed and Robbie slipped his arm around each woman's waist. He closed his eyes and sighed.

"What does that mean?" Sadie's voice trembled and Robbie squeezed her.

The doctor looked up at them. "I must be honest. There isn't anything I can do for Jack. This isn't the kind of tumor I can just take out. I believe it's in his blood. I'm afraid it's just a matter of time."

"Ohhhhhhh." The two women clung to each other and sobbed, Robbie held them tightly, and both put their heads on his shoulders.

His heart was doing somersaults. He couldn't bear to see either of them hurt. He leaned his head against Sadie's. "I'm so sorry," he whispered, quite unable to believe how much compassion he felt.

At last, Beth took a breath and sat up. "How long, Doc?"

"There's no way to really know. I've seen some people go really quickly from the outset of symptoms; others have lived several months. He's otherwise healthy and strong."

"Can he come home?" Sadie's voice trembled. Robbie felt his heart shattering. He couldn't believe how much he ached for a family he'd just met. It was a new feeling, so much compassion for people. He was shocked to realize he'd come to love them very much even in the short time he'd known them. He'd wanted a family for so long. He gasped internally. *It appears Sadie was right. I do have a family.* Despite the pain in his heart at seeing these women hurting, he smiled. It was thrilling to have them rely on him, it felt natural, and his heart longed for more.

The doctor gave them a kind smile. "I don't know, Mrs. Nelson, he's going to be in pain, and I think we ought to keep him here, at least for now. That way, I can keep an eye on him, and keep him comfortable. When he wakes, we'll take him to one of the private recovery rooms. It has two beds so you can stay there with him."

"What's going to happen to his livery? We need to survive?" Ever practical, Beth squeezed Jack's hand.

Sadie sat up and gasped. She turned and put her hand on Robbie's arm. "Robbie."

Robbie frowned and Beth raised her brows to Sadie.

"What are you saying?" Robbie murmured.

"You could run the livery. You said it was always your dream to run a livery. You can take over for Uncle Jack." Her eyes lit up, and her trust in him made his heart lurch. "It's the ideal solution."

Robbie frowned. "I'm not so sure. I don't think I know how to run a livery."

Sadie turned around and gripped his arm. "Yes, you can. We can. I'll help you."

He raised his brows and gestured to her arm.

"This won't be forever, and there are lots of things I can do for you in the meantime, like maybe the paperwork." She raised her brows to him.

"That would be wonderful, Robbie. Would you consider it?" Beth's face pleaded.

Robbie sighed. "I was planning to leave town...."

Sadie put her hand on his cheek. "Please don't leave. We need you. You're family, and we need you. I'll help you as much as I can." Her eyes flooded with tears and she marvelled internally at how attached she felt to him.

Robbie bit his lip. Her hand was so soft against his cheek, and it made his heart ache. He looked at both sets of pleading eyes, exhaled loudly and shrugged. "If you really think I can do it?"

Sadie's lip trembled and she threw her uninjured arm around his neck. He gasped and put his hand on her back. Every time he held her, his heart fluttered in his chest.

"Thank you, Robbie. I'm so glad you aren't going to leave."

He nodded. "I'll stay for a time, while I work out what I'm going to do and to help you all adjust. But I make no promises in the long term."

"That's all we ask, Robbie." Beth embraced him. "We'll do much better with you to look out for us."

"That's good news, Robbie." The Doctor smiled. "Jack will be pleased to know his livery is in good hands."

"I'm not so sure about that. I don't really know what I'm doing, but I can learn. I've worked in liveries before but never on my own." Robbie ran his fingers through his hair and sighed.

"We can send away for some books on animal husbandry for you and running a livery. There are plenty of volumes available," the doctor suggested.

Robbie's cheeks reddened and he opened his mouth to say something, but Sadie took over. "That's great. We can work it out together."

He nodded and gulped. "I'll need your help. And God's."

Sadie smiled and squeezed his hand. "I'd be happy to. I've been working with Uncle Jack in the livery anyway." She put her hand on his chest. "I'm so pleased you'll get to live out one of your dreams. I hope you fulfill them all and truly find a home here." She lowered her eyes. "And a family of your own."

The doctor smiled. The looks in both sets of eyes told him all he needed to know. Robbie likely didn't know it yet, but it was obvious he was in love with Sadie.

A groan came from the bed and the doctor jumped to attention as Jack began to come round. He stirred some powder into a cup of water, ready to give him pain relief.

Thirteen

"Thank you for agreeing to take on my livery." Jack's voice was raspy and weak. "It'll bring me much comfort if you could take care of my girls." He winked at Sadie and put his hand out to Beth.

Robbie swallowed and gulped. "I... Uhhhh... I don't know.... I uhhh... I don't know how to care for a family... I..." His voice petered out.

"You'll work it out, Son. I'm proud of you for how you took care of my Sadie. Thank you for saving her life." Jack coughed slightly. Even talking was painful.

"The only promise I can make is I'll do my best." Robbie's voice trembled.

"That's all I ask; all you have to do is love them with all your heart."

Robbie nodded and squeezed the older man's shoulder. "You have my word."

Jack gave Robbie a single nod and his eyes reflected his deep gratitude.

"How are you feeling today?"

Before Jack could answer the doctor's question, the sheriff walked in and stood shuffling his feet and twisting his hat in his hands.

"Sheriff, what brings you here?" The doctor walked over to shake his hand. Robbie nodded to him.

"I'm sorry to have to do this, but I'm afraid, I have to arrest Robbie."

Robbie's face fell. Sadie gasped, leaped up out of her chair and gripped Robbie's arm. "Why? What has he done?"

The sheriff took a deep breath and flicked his hair back from his forehead. "I've had a report of inappropriate conduct."

Robbie frowned.

"The two of you spent five nights together in a cabin in the woods, and you are unmarried. I've also been told you removed Sadie's clothing when she was asleep." The sheriff's face gave away his extreme regret.

"Just her dress, Sir, to save her life. Nothing inappropriate happened in that cabin; I can assure you of that."

"It's true, Sheriff." Sadie clutched the arm of the man she was falling in love with. "He was nothing but a gentleman. He treated me with dignity and respect. Nothing inappropriate happened; if he'd left me in that wet dress, I might've got pneumonia. He did not remove any other layers, and I remained covered up the entire time. I don't press any charges, Sheriff." Sadie gave Robbie's arm a squeeze to reassure him she didn't hold it against him.

The sheriff shook his head. "I'm sorry, Miss Nelson. It's been reported, and the person reporting is worried for your reputation." He turned to look at Robbie. "I'm afraid I have to take you in." He grimaced. "I'm sorry. I think the charges are ludicrous, and I hope we can come to some kind of arrangement, but the person seemed adamant they'd take it further if I don't arrest you. They threatened to call in the US Marshalls. If that happens, it's beyond my jurisdiction."

Robbie shook his head. "Fine, I'll come in." He turned to follow the sheriff out of the room.

"Noooo. You can't arrest him. He didn't do anything wrong." Sadie ran over and gripped Robbie's arm.

"It's okay, Sadie, we'll work it out. I promise. You stay here with Aunt Beth. She needs you." He gripped her shoulder.

Sadie stood up on her toes and kissed Robbie's cheek. "And I need you." She held his gaze for a time, attempting to communicate her feelings for him. Her lip trembled and tears pooled in the corners of her eyes.

Robbie looked at her and a wry smile crossed his face. *What does she mean by that?* He embraced her gently so as not to hurt her arm. "I'll be fine, Sadie. We'll work this out. I promise," he whispered in her ear.

Sadie wiped at her tears. "Can I come by and see him?"

"Of course." The sheriff nodded.

"I'll be by tomorrow." She gripped Robbie's arm. She desperately wanted to tell him she loved him but couldn't squeeze the words past her throat. Besides, she didn't yet know how he felt about her.

Robbie nodded and let the sheriff lead him away.

From her vantage point in one of the other cubicles, Miss Neville nodded her head. "I should think so. How absolutely scandalous. Five nights in a cabin in the woods, and them not married. What was he thinking? And to remove her clothing.... Why he ought to be hung for such behavior."

Sadie and Aunt Beth clung to each other by Jack's bed and wept. "It's not fair." Beth clung to her niece.

"I know, Aunty. Robbie did nothing wrong. He was only ever the gentleman. He looked after me and treated me kindly. Nothing at all inappropriate took place."

"I know, Darling." Aunt Beth patted her hand. "I know that he's a good man, and I know he'd never hurt you. He couldn't; he's a Gordon."

Sadie sat back. "It's so sad. He doesn't believe he deserves a family or is even capable of having one. He deserves it more than anyone after missing out for twenty-one years." She lifted her handkerchief to her eyes.

Aunt Beth noticed the glow to her eyes and the complete turnaround in her feelings towards Robbie. She knew he hadn't done anything inappropriate in the cabin, but something had certainly changed. She smiled, patted Sadie's hand, and looked her in the eye. "Then it's up to you to convince him, Darling."

"What are you saying, Aunt Beth?"

Beth tucked a strand of hair behind Sadie's ear. "You ought to show him that he can't live without you." She winked at her.

Sadie blushed. "Oh, Aunty, I'm so confused. He has me all twisted up in knots."

Beth smiled. "Love does that."

"Love?" Sadie frowned. "I never said anything about love." But the reddening of her cheeks said otherwise.

Beth kissed her niece, grinned, and gripped her hand tightly. "I couldn't think of a single thing that would make me happier than to see you and Robbie as a happy family."

Sadie tucked her lips under. "Isn't it a bit weird? We're kind of cousins."

"Not at all. You have no blood in common; you yourself assured me of that. I think it's wonderful, Sadie." Beth gushed.

"You're getting ahead of yourself, Aunty. It's not me you need to convince."

Beth frowned.

"He's planning to leave town after a while. He still thinks he's better off alone."

"Then change his mind, Sadie."

Sadie nodded. "I'll try." She couldn't keep the shy smile off her face. "But I don't know how he feels about me?"

Beth raised her brows and nodded. *He's deeply in love with you, Girl, and he'll see it in time.*

*   *   *   *

"I'm sorry to have to do this, Robbie. You know if I had my way, I'd let you out. I know you did nothing wrong." The sheriff shook his head and scratched his chin.

Robbie nodded and sat back on the bed in the cell. He looked at the sheriff. "I understand; you're just doing your job. I could never hurt Sadie... any woman for that matter." He covered himself quickly.

The sheriff noticed the wry smile, and an idea formed in his mind. He locked the cell door. "I'll have Missy from the café bring you meals, and if you need the outhouse, let me know, and I'll escort you."

"Thank you. I appreciate it."

"You want something to read while you're there?"

"No, but there is one thing I need."

The sheriff nodded. "I'll look after your dog. He can sleep in with me."

"Good, Sadie isn't really a fan of dogs."

The sheriff grinned. *Funny how she's his first thought.*

Robbie shrugged. "What will happen to the livery with me in here?"

"It won't hurt for it to be closed for a few more days."

Robbie nodded. "How long will I have to be here?"

The sheriff shook his head. "I can't say. I need to speak to the person who pressed charges, and see if we can come up with a solution."

"Who was it?"

"A woman in the clinic. She was in the next cubicle when you brought Sadie in and overheard your conversation."

Robbie nodded. "It's just as well. I was starting to think long-term. I ought to know better."

"What are you saying?"

"It was starting to feel like I might be putting down roots here." Robbie shrugged. "But this just confirms that I ought to leave town."

"That's an option I suppose, but where does that leave Sadie and Beth?"

"What do you mean?" Robbie ran his fingers through his hair.

"Jack's not expected to live. Then what?"

Robbie closed his eyes and shook his head. "I don't know."

The sheriff raised his brows. "You wanted a family. It looks like you've got one."

Robbie sighed and closed his eyes. "I can't. I'm not equipped to be in a family. I don't know how. I've been alone for far too long."

The sheriff merely nodded.

*　*　*　*

"How are you getting on?" Sadie's eyes searched Robbie's face through the bars.

"I'm alright, I suppose." He shrugged, trying desperately to force down his growing feelings. He could not let himself fall for her, no matter how much his heart longed for her. He'd been shocked at the depth of his feelings as he lay awake staring at the ceiling overnight. The sheriff's words rang in his ears, and he couldn't help but wonder if he was right. He'd spent a lot of time praying God would take the feelings from him. It'd just bring hurt.

"Do you need anything?"

"No. Thank you." He sat back on the bed.

"Robbie?" Sadie frowned. "Don't shut me out."

He sighed and stood and walked up to the bars. "I'm not, Sadie. I'm just being honest."

She searched his eyes. "You still mean to leave?"

"This just confirms it." Robbie gestured to the cell. "When I try to do the right thing for family…" He pointed to her. "I just make a mess of everything. I'm better off alone. I told you that."

Sadie burst into tears. "Oh, Robbie, won't you please stay? I need you. Aunt Beth needs you. What's going to happen to us when Uncle Jack dies?"

Robbie closed his eyes and sighed. He dropped his chin to his chest for a time. "Don't put that pressure on me. I told you, I don't know how to have a family. I'll just let you all down."

Sadie put her hand through the bars to touch his shoulder. "Yes, you do. Search your heart. I've come to depend on you. It's scary, I never thought I'd depend on anyone. But I've realized I depend on you. We depend on you, Me, and Aunt Beth."

Robbie's heart ached. More than anything he wanted to give her his heart, love her, and be a family, but he was so certain he'd ruin everything and leave her and Aunt Beth miserable. He sighed and closed his eyes. "Sadie." He exhaled the word.

She nodded and dropped the subject. "I still want to teach you to read and write."

"Can't do that in here." He shrugged.

Sadie gripped his arm again. "Well, I plan to get you out soon, and then I'll teach you."

"Where am I supposed to go? I don't work at the Circle A anymore. I guess I can go to the boarding house, but my meagre savings won't last long."

"You'll come and live with us. We have plenty of space."

Robbie frowned. "Sadie, that wouldn't be appropriate. That's kinda what got me in trouble in the first place."

"But you're family, and Aunt Beth will be there."

"We're not blood, Sadie. I'm not really your family. It would be inappropriate for a single man to live there with you there. I think we've brought enough scandal on ourselves. Nah, I'm better off going back to roaming. Me and Ozzie do better on our own."

"I promise we'll work this out. I'm even starting to come to terms with Ozzie."

Robbie nodded. "You should get back to Aunt Beth. She needs you."

Sadie tried to keep the disappointment from registering in her eyes. She sniffed. "I'll be by tomorrow. I'll bring the Bible, and I can read to you if you'd like that."

"Sure." He shrugged. "How's your wrist?"

"Sore, but the doctor's given me pain relief and it's improving."

"How long?"

"He said at least another week. He doesn't think it's a bad break, perhaps just a fracture but he wants to keep it firmly splinted for now, so it heals. I'll have to be careful for a time and keep it strapped to make sure it stays strong."

Robbie gripped her hand. "It'll heal quickly. I'll pray for you." He grimaced internally. *Why did I say that?* Just recently, he'd found himself drawing near to God. He just wished he could read the words for himself. He repeated the scriptures he knew by heart as often as he could, but he knew without being able to read, he couldn't really grow in his faith.

Sadie shrugged. "I better go."

"Thanks for coming to visit."

"Of course."

He watched as she walked out of the room, then sighed loudly and fell back on the bed. He could no longer deny his feelings for her. His heart ached whenever he saw her, and he wanted nothing more than wrap her in his arms and kiss her. Her lips looked so soft and enticing, he longed to know what they'd feel like against his. To stay in Dusty Ridge and have a family with her would be bliss. Sometimes he convinced himself it was possible, but then the old insecurities would come back. "What kind of a husband would I be? I can't read, have no money, no way to really provide, no home, and no idea how to be a husband and a spiritual leader that she needs. How can I do that if I can't even read?"

Trust me, for I know the thoughts I think towards you... Robbie gasped. The voice had felt so real. "God?" He scratched his chin. "Is that You? Please show me the way You want me to go?"

Fourteen

"I've called you all here to talk about your options." The sheriff eyed Sadie and Beth, who sat outside the cell, then turned to look at Robbie.

"Options?" Robbie raised his brows and perched on the edge of his bed. He'd been in jail almost a week now, and he was becoming frustrated. Jack was getting weaker, and the pain on Aunt Beth's and Sadie's faces made him ache. He wished he could be free of his cell to support them.

"I've spoken to Miss Neville, and she's agreed to drop the charges on one of two conditions."

Sadie grinned. "Oh, whatever they are, Robbie will do them. He needs to get out of there." She blushed and turned to look at Robbie. "Sorry for speaking for you."

He smiled, glad to know she cared. "S'okay." He turned to the sheriff. "Conditions?"

"She claims she's only thinking of Sadie's reputation. Apparently, there's been some gossip. I imagine Miss Neville stirred up that gossip herself. There's no one else it could've come from. She does enjoy a good scandal." The sheriff shook his head. "Anyhow, to save Miss Nelson's reputation, you have two options that would satisfy Miss Neville. Either leave town, and never come back…."

Sadie gasped and let out a sob. She closed her eyes as she felt her heart breaking.

Robbie nodded. "I've already considered that. It might be better for everyone if I did, for Sadie's sake." He shrugged, his heart lurched, and it surprised him to realize how much that idea caused him to ache.

"What's the other option?" Sadie asked.

The sheriff raised his brows and looked from Sadie to Robbie. "That you get married."

"Ohhhh." Sadie's cheeks reddened. She tucked her lips under and stared at her hands in her lap, hoping Robbie couldn't hear the screaming of her heart. *Oh, yes, let's do that. I wouldn't mind.*

Robbie felt his heart flip. *If only that was possible.* He was surprised at the longing in his heart. "Oh... well... I don't know." He blushed and scratched at his chin.

Beth clasped her hands together and grinned. She gripped Sadie's arm. "That's ideal. I couldn't think of a better solution. You two could be so happy together. You can live in our home and run the livery. And live happily ever after."

Robbie's heart began to race, and his cheeks warmed. *Nothing would make me happier.* He swallowed and shook his head. "I dunno. I'm sure you're all better off if I just leave town."

Sadie said nothing, but Aunt Beth caught the slight tremble of her lips.

The sheriff nodded. "It's your decision, Robbie." He turned to the ladies. "Let's leave him to consider it."

"When do I have to decide?"

"Tomorrow morning. Or I'll have to have you transported to the county prison to face charges, can't keep you here indefinitely."

Robbie sighed. He nodded and lifted his knees onto the bed.

Sadie and Beth followed the sheriff out. Sadie gave him a shy smile. *Oh Lord, I sure would be keen to marry him.* She blushed deeply. *I couldn't bear to have him leave town. I need him. I don't want to be without him.* She shook her head slightly, amused at her own change of tune.

*   *   *   *

Robbie wrestled with the options in his mind. The thought of marrying Sadie filled his heart with delight. How wonderful it would be to work alongside her in the livery and have a family with her. Never being alone again. Nothing would thrill him more than to have a family and a home for the rest of his days, with that incredible woman. *But ohhh, how can I do that? How can I be the man and leader she needs me to be when I have no idea how to even be a part of a family, and I can't even read or write. I have nothing at all to offer a woman like Sadie.* He sighed loudly and spoke to the air. "What do I do, Lord? Is this You telling me it's time to move on?"

For I know the thoughts I think towards you... He gasped; there was that voice again. "What do You mean, God?"

Trust in the Lord with all thine heart; and lean not unto thine own understanding. In all thy ways acknowledge Him, and He shall direct thy paths. The verse Mrs. Bonnie had quoted many times rang in his ears. "I do trust You, God. I just don't have anything to offer her. She'd end up disappointed in me." He said aloud. "I don't know how to have a family." He sighed loudly and buried his face in his hands.

"Yes, you do."

Robbie snapped his head up to see Sadie and the sheriff. "What are you doing here?" He stood and walked to the bars. *She's so beautiful. If only it was possible...* he sighed.

"I asked Sheriff Carr to bring me here so I could talk to you." Sadie turned to him. "Can I go in to talk to him?"

"I'll have to lock you in." The sheriff lifted the keys and gestured to the lock.

"That'll be fine." Sadie smiled.

"I'll be in the office. Call out when you want out." The sheriff opened the cell and let Sadie in, locking the door behind her.

"Thank you, Sheriff. I'll call out."

He nodded and walked out, leaving the door to his office ajar.

"Why are you here?" Robbie looked up at her.

She sat on the end of his bed. "I wanted to talk to you."

"Why?" He sat down beside her.

"I know you're struggling to make a decision."

He shrugged. "I think it's best I just leave."

"Best for whom?"

"All of us."

Sadie squinted at him. "Are you deciding what's best for me without actually consulting me?"

"What're you saying?"

She moved closer to him and he turned to look at her. She lifted a hand to his cheek. "I don't want you to leave."

Robbie sighed and looked at his feet. "I don't want to either."

She smiled. "Then don't."

"Then we'd have to get married." He shrugged.

Sadie blushed. "Is that such a bad thing?" Her voice was quiet and full of emotion.

Robbie explored her face intently. "Sadie, I'd marry you in a heartbeat if I thought it was the right thing to do. Nothing would thrill me more," he confessed out loud.

Her heart leaped for joy, and she tried desperately to keep the grin from her face. "What's the hesitation?"

He stood and walked to the bars, turning his back to her. "I'm not husband material."

"Why not?"

"I don't know how to be a husband or lead a family. I don't know how to be the man you need me to be. I'm so woefully inadequate at that." He turned to look at her. "I can't even read."

Sadie stood up. "What does any of that have to do with getting married?"

"You need a better man than me. You deserve so much better." He shrugged. "I'm a loner."

"Robbie. You're the best man I know."

He squinted at her. "Are you saying you want to get married?" The flutter in his heart caught him off guard and he inhaled sharply. *I know the thoughts that I think toward you....* the voice said again.

She looked up at him, her cheeks flushed deeply, and she gave him a shy smile. "I'd be open to it."

He closed his eyes and sighed, leaning back against the bars. "I'm scared, Sadie."

"Scared of what?"

"I told you a thousand times. I have no idea how to have a family..."

Sadie put a finger to his lips to stop him. "You know how to love. That's all a family is." He frowned, so she smiled and continued. "Out there in that cabin, you were so gentle and kind, so loving and caring. That's what being a family is. That's how you be a husband. You already know the most important thing, and that is how to love. That's the one thing you can't learn how to do."

He sighed. "But you don't want a stupid husband who can't even read. How am I supposed to lead spiritually if I can't even read the Bible with you? How can I have a business to support a family if I can't read and write." He shrugged.

Sadie wasn't giving up so easily. "Robbie, you aren't stupid and there's more to providing than reading and writing. There's more to leading than reading Scripture. Besides, I'm confident that's a temporary measure, and you'll learn in no time. You're plenty smart enough."

"Do you really think so?"

She smiled. "I know so." She put a hand on his chest and looked up at him. "Even if you never learned to read and write, I've already come to rely on you so much. I never thought I'd ever depend on a man. I thought that it would make me weak. But I've felt so much stronger in the last few weeks than I've felt in my whole life. Having you to depend on is like a dream come true. If you never learn to read, then I'll do the reading for you. If you never learn to write, then I'll help you in your business."

"Are you sure this is what you want?" His heart was doing hopeful somersaults.

"Only if you love me. If you don't, then leave. I don't want to be in a marriage of convenience."

"I do love you," Robbie murmured under his breath.

Sadie's heart flipped again. "What was that?" She bit her lips together.

Trust Me, I AM with you. That voice again. Robbie took a deep breath and exhaled all his fear and worry. He turned to look into Sadie's eyes. He smiled and cupped her cheek. "I do love you. I'm certain I'll always love you. I'd like to marry you, if you'll have me, with all my flaws." He closed his eyes. His whole body trembled. He'd never been so vulnerable in all his life.

Sadie touched his cheek, and he opened his eyes. "Of course, I'll have you. I love you too."

"You will? You do?" His eyes lit up.

"On one condition."

He frowned.

"That you ask me properly, when you get a ring."

He raised his brows, grinned, walked to the other side of the cell, picked up his knapsack, and rummaged through it.

Sadie put her hand on her hip and frowned.

He found what he needed and walked to her. He knelt and lifted his mother's ring to her.

She gasped. "Where did you get that?"

"It's the only thing I have of my mother's other than the New Testament."

"Oohhhh." She put her hands over her mouth.

Robbie reached for her hand, and his whole body shook. "Sadie. I have nothing to offer you, apart from all the love in my heart and that in abundance."

"That's all I want. The rest we can just work out together." Her eyes shone with love for him.

He was still not certain she wouldn't live to regret it, but his heart was bursting. *Trust Me.* The voice prompted him. He smiled. "Sadie Nelson. I love you. Will you be my wife?" He exhaled deeply as all the fear and doubt left his heart. *Lord, I'm gonna need Your help.*

"Of course, I'll marry you. I love you too."

Robbie stood up and gave her a wide smile. He put a large hand on her soft cheek. "You're so beautiful. You have no idea how badly I wanted to kiss you when I brushed your hair in that cabin. It took all the willpower I had to resist." He searched her face with his eyes for a time.

Sadie raised shining eyes to look at him, and put her good hand on his chest. "You don't have to resist now."

He nodded, brushed her cheek, then pulled her close and bent his head to kiss her. She slipped her right arm around his neck and gave her all in that kiss.

Just at that moment, Aunt Beth and the sheriff walked in. Both looked at each other and grinned.

Sheriff Carr coughed twice and they broke apart abruptly, both faces a deep red.

Aunt Beth gushed and clasped her hands together. Sadie bit her bottom lip and gave Robbie a shy smile.

Robbie winked at her and put his hand on her back.

The sheriff raised his brows. He grinned at the pair. "It looks to me like you've made a decision."

Robbie nodded and reached for Sadie's hand. She gave his a supportive squeeze.

"I know nothing about being a husband or having a family. But this beautiful woman has convinced me we can learn that together. I just hope you don't live to regret it." He grimaced.

"Never." Sadie was determined.

Aunt Beth's eyes filled with tears, and she clapped. "Oh, this is the most wonderful news. Ohhhh." She put a hand out to both as the sheriff unlocked the cell. "Ohhh, Jack will be so delighted."

"And, Aunt Beth. I'll take on the livery if you still want me to...." Robbie winked at Sadie. "Course I'll need the help of..." He grinned. "My wife when she's healed." *Wife. That word seems so strange but so right.*

Beth threw her arms around Robbie and kissed his cheek. "I'm so excited about this. God has brought the right man for our Sadie, and I couldn't be more thrilled. I'm so happy for the two of you."

"Thanks, Aunt Beth."

She stepped back and embraced Sadie. "I'm so proud of you," she whispered in her ear. "For being willing to depend on someone."

Robbie overheard. "I'll depend on her too."

Beth gripped both shoulders. "You must get married right away. I'll move my things to the guest room, and you must take over our bedroom."

"Aunt Beth, there's no need. We have time to work these things out."

"I know that Jack will never come home." Her lips trembled and she wiped away a tear. "But he would want this. If I can't have him anymore, then I'll be thrilled to have the two of you there with me. Of course, I'd be happy to move to the boarding house, and you can have our home next to the livery."

Robbie frowned. "I wouldn't dream of it." He looked at Sadie and she grinned.

"Aunt Beth, we want you to stay. We won't kick you out of your own home," Sadie insisted.

"It's just a house. Without Jack, it's little more than wood." Beth shrugged. "But you will bring joy to the house again. I really will move out if that's what you want."

Robbie gripped her shoulder. "No. I don't know how to have a family, but I do know I want to work it out more than anything in this world. I've always longed for a home and family, and a place to belong. I'm absolutely terrified that I'll get it all wrong and ruin everything, but Sadie assures me we can work this out together. So, if you'll have me in your family, Aunt Beth, I'd sure like to try."

"Nothing would make me happier."

"Well then. I'd better give you this." Robbie turned to Sadie, lifted her hand, and slipped the ring on. It fitted perfectly.

Beth's eyes filled with tears, and she gasped.

Sadie touched her arm. "What is it?"

"I helped my brother choose that ring for Pearl. It even has a pearl on it."

Sadie lifted it. "It's beautiful."

"I'm glad you like it. I've carried it with me all these years, and I always hoped I'd have the chance to give it to the woman I loved, although I was scared to do so."

"Well, what are we waiting for? We have a wedding to organize." Beth gushed.

Robbie winked at Sadie and lowered his head to kiss her again. "Can't wait."

"Me either. I know exactly the dress I'm going to wear."

Robbie grimaced. "I'm afraid I don't have anything special to wear."

"I don't care about that. Just wear your Sunday things."

"Okay. So, when do you want to do this?" His whole body was alive with overwhelming joy.

Sadie looked at her aunt.

Beth smiled. "I can have the house ready for you in a few hours. I'll get Maisy Turner to help me."

"Okay, how about tomorrow at noon, and we can have our wedding luncheon at the café with whoever from the church wants to come."

"And the ranch hands. I'd like them there."

"Great." Sadie squeezed Robbie's hand. "I'm just sorry my hand won't get better in time."

"Don't be sorry, I'll be happy to help you when you need me. It'd be my pleasure." He winked.

Sadie gave him a wide smile and leaned back into him.

"Can he leave now, Sheriff?" Beth asked.

"Yes, but if you don't go through with this, I'll have to arrest you again."

"Thank you, Sheriff. I'll be there." Robbie grinned and they walked out. "Now, I need to go and have a conversation with Uncle Jack. Is he awake?"

"Yes." Beth smiled. "That's what I was coming to tell you; he's awake and feeling good today. Oh, this will thrill him." She turned to Robbie and became very serious. "And then you'll have to make yourself scarce. You can't see the bride until your wedding. We'll have the house ready for you both to move into tomorrow. I'll bring my things and stay with your uncle in his room at the clinic until he passes. I've been doing that most nights anyway. Give you newlyweds time to get to know each other."

Sadie and Robbie gave each other shy smiles.

"Alright, I'll sleep at the ranch tonight. I'm sure they can give me a bunk for the night. I want to invite them all anyway, and talk to Turner about the horse farm."

"I'm sorry that you don't get to do that."

"It's fine, Sadie. I like the idea of working with my wife in the livery."

"Until you have children." Beth gushed. "Oh, I can't wait. It'll be like having grandchildren."

"Aunt Beth," Sadie scolded. "One thing at a time."

Beth chuckled. "Well, I'll give you two a few moments alone. We'll see to the arrangements, Robbie. I'll see you at the church at noon tomorrow."

"I'll be there, Aunt Beth."

Beth and the sheriff left the room for a moment. Robbie turned to Sadie. He took her one good hand in both of his large ones. He fixed his eyes on hers. "Are you absolutely sure, you are willing to take on this roaming loner and teach him how to be a husband?"

She stood up on her toes and kissed him deeply, prolonging it for as long as she could. When she stepped back from him, his eyes glowed, and he wore a wide smile. "I'll take that as a yes."

"And so, you should." She grinned. "I can't wait for you to be my husband."

Robbie stroked her cheek. "I'll see you at noon. I've longed for this for a long time, but I never imagined it would ever happen for me. I truly thought I'd spend my life alone and roaming."

"Well, you're never going to be alone again. I'm afraid, Mr. Gordon, you're stuck with me for the rest of your days."

He grinned and winked at her. "Can't wait."

She stood up and kissed him again. "See you at the church tomorrow." She turned and walked away.

He watched her walk out, grinned, picked up his knapsack, and paused for a moment. "Thank You, Lord. But I sure am gonna need Your help." He whistled to Ozzie and headed out.

Fifteen

Robbie took a seat next to Uncle Jack's bed. The man was sitting up. He was frail but alert.

"Hi, Son. I'm glad to see you're out of jail. It wasn't fair what happened. Sadie explained it all to me. I know you did what you had to, to save her life, and I'm grateful to you."

"Thanks." Robbie was visibly nervous.

"And I wanted to thank you again for saving my Sadie. I can't believe the change in her. She's softened and blossomed. You got her to be vulnerable, and I like what I see. It makes me happy to know she's in good hands." He raised his brows knowingly.

"I wanted to talk to you about that, Sir." Robbie swallowed. "I know this has been rather hurried, and our hands have been somewhat forced, but I can't say I'm sorry. I love her, and I want to ask for your blessing to marry Sadie."

Jack lifted a weak arm to grip his shoulder. "Nothing would make me happier. I'm overjoyed to know you'll be here for my family when I can't be." He shuddered.

"I'm sorry about that, Uncle Jack."

"Don't be. I go to be with my Lord. I'm just sorry to leave my girls."

"I'll do my utmost to watch out for both of them. I give you my word."

"You'll do just fine, Robbie. I couldn't think of a better man for our Sadie. Her father would've been thrilled. I know with you, my girls will be in good hands.”

“Thank you. I’m not as confident as you. I’ve been alone for so long....”

“You don’t want a family?”

“I want a family more than anything. And the fact that I get that with Sadie....” Robbie’s face lit up. “Is thrilling. I can’t wait to spend my life with her.”

“Then that’s all you need, and you don’t need to be worried. Just trust the Lord and love her with all your heart. That’s all you have to do.”

“I will, Sir, and I’ll do my best with your livery.”

“You’ll do fine, Son. Let Sadie help you; she’s shrewd and clever.”

“I’ll need her, too. Couldn’t do it without her.”

The doctor walked in. “I couldn’t help but overhear. Congratulations.” He put his hand out to Robbie.

Robbie stood and shook the doctor’s hand. “Thank you.”

“There’s a shine in your eyes.”

“Never thought I’d ever get to be so blessed. It may have been a little sudden and in unusual circumstances, but I know God orchestrated it.”

“He did,” Jack determined.

The doctor squeezed Robbie’s shoulder. “I know it wasn’t what you planned, but you obviously love each other and take it as an unexpected blessing. There’s nothing like a good marriage, Gordon. Enjoy it.”

“I will. I wanted to ask you a question, if you don’t mind.”

“Ask away.” The doctor nodded.

"Is there any possibility Jack could walk Sadie down the aisle?"

The doctor looked at Jack. "If he feels strong enough. Of course, he'd need to be in a wheelchair until then and come right back to bed afterward."

"Nothing would thrill me more. I'll be strong enough, I promise. I wouldn't miss this for the world." Jack beamed.

"Excellent. Noon tomorrow." Robbie raised his brows and grinned at the pair.

"I'll have him there," the doctor assured him.

*　*　*　*

"You ready for this?" Jerry chuckled as he watched Robbie taking deep breaths as they waited at the front of the church.

"Yes."

"That doesn't sound convincing. Are you having second thoughts?"

"Not about Sadie. She's amazing. Just about my ability to be a husband."

"You'll be an excellent husband." A man walked in the door.

Robbie looked up; his mouth fell open, and turned to a wide smile. "Tim? What're you doing here?"

"Got a telegram yesterday saying my best friend was getting married. I couldn't let you get married without me."

"But who..." Robbie was struck speechless as he embraced his friend.

151

"Your bride sent a telegram to Colorado Springs. I got my fastest horse. Takes five hours in the saddle at a hard gallop. Poor horse, I about wore him out."

"And how long are you staying?"

"Long enough for lunch. Gotta get back to Maisy and the mill."

"I'm glad you came." Robbie swiped at a tear.

Tim grinned. "Well, you stood up with me at my wedding; I wanted to return the favor."

Robbie turned to Jerry and grimaced. "I can have both of you."

Jerry slapped Robbie's back. "I'm more than happy to pass the mantle to your friend. I'm just glad to be here to watch. I remember saying I felt sorry for the man who'd end up with Sadie. I take that back."

Robbie laughed. "It's fine. I've got to know her, and she's not what she appeared at first glance. I'm sure that was a cover-up for her tender heart." He grinned widely.

Tim slapped his friends' back. "I can tell by your eyes that you're a lucky man, Rob. I'm pleased for ya."

"Thanks, Tim. I'm glad you're here. I was gonna send you a wire, but I never dreamed you'd make it in time. The circumstances were rather hurried. I'm so touched that Sadie did that for me."

"You know, I'd say she really loves you."

Robbie shook his head and scratched at his clean-shaven chin. "Never thought I'd see the day. I was sure I'd roam my whole life."

"Hey, if I can settle down, so can you."

Robbie became serious. "How'd ya do it?"

"What do you mean?"

"How'd you adjust after being alone for so long, get used to having a family?"

"I was terrified I'd not be any good. That I'd let Maisy down every day. But the moment I woke up with that woman in my arms, it was so natural. I felt like I'd been there with her my whole life." He shrugged. "Can't remember what life was like before. I can assure you, in a week's time, you'll wonder what you were ever worried about. Just love her. That's all you have to do."

"I can do that. Thank you, my friend." Robbie grinned as the pastor arrived and people began appearing. The crew from the Circle A would be there soon.

"Mr. Gordon, your bride will be here soon." The pastor smiled.

Robbie grinned widely. "Can't quite believe it."

Tim frowned at him.

"What?" Robbie asked.

"Gordon?" Tim raised his brows.

"I finally found out who I am, Tim. I'm Robbie Gordon."

"How'd you find out?"

"Turns out my aunt lives in this town. She recognized me. Evidently, I look like my father, her brother. She'd heard I'd died at birth. She's how I met Sadie."

Tim raised his brows, encouraging Robbie to explain.

"Sadie is the niece of Aunt Beth's husband. They raised her."

"Well, you've fallen on your feet. I'm glad. I've been praying for you and wondering where you are."

"I'll be taking on Uncle Jack's livery too. With my bride's help."

Tim embraced his friend. "I'm proud of you, Rob."

"Thanks, Tim. I'm looking forward to writing to Mrs. Bonnie to let her know."

Tim patted his back. "She'll be proud."

Beth walked up and embraced Robbie. "I'm so proud of you, Robbie. My brother would be proud of the man you've become, despite all you've been through."

"Thanks, Aunt Beth, I hope so. I have my father's pocket watch with me. I feel like he's watching."

"He is, absolutely."

"Aunt Beth, this is my best friend, Tim. We've been together since our days in the orphanage."

"Tim. It's nice to meet you. Sadie told me she was sending you a wire."

Tim greeted her. "Ma'am, nice to meet you. I'm glad to hear Rob has a family at last. It's all he ever wanted."

"We're thrilled." Beth turned to Robbie, gripping both his shoulders. "Sadie's all ready. She'll be here very soon. I better go and help Jack."

Robbie's face lit up and he took a deep breath. "Thanks, Aunt Beth, I can't wait."

The pianist began to play and the congregation took their seats. Mr. Turner and Mr. Baker walked in with the rest of the Circle A crew. Robbie gave them a nod. The two men walked up and shook his hand. "Proud of you, Robbie." Sam slapped his back.

"Thank you, Mr. Turner, Mr. Baker. If it weren't for you giving me the chance, I'd not be standing here today."

"It's our pleasure, Lad. Nothing better than seeing a man take an opportunity and make something of himself," Baker offered.

Mr. Turner grinned. "Saw your bride outside. She's glowing."

Robbie exhaled loudly. The two men chuckled and joined their wives and the cowboys in their seats. The bridal march started to play, and Robbie took deep breaths. Sadie appeared in the doorway on Uncle Jack's arm.

Tears flooded Robbie's eyes and he shook his head. He dropped his hands to his knees and sniffed back his tears.

Tim grinned and gripped his shoulders. "Just breathe, my friend. She's something."

"She's.... Ohhh. She's...." Robbie couldn't get the words out. He shook his head and straightened up. His heart threatened to explode from his chest as he watched Sadie walk toward them.

He was unable to draw his eyes from her beaming face. She wore a dusky pink dress and had foregone the sling for the day. She held a bunch of wildflowers and had more tucked into her hair.

Robbie's eyes ached with the sight of her. He took three deep breaths, and by the time she reached the altar he was weeping.

"Breathe." Tim leaned in. "You're a blessed man."

Robbie nodded, took a deep breath, and grinned at Sadie.

"Who gives this woman to be married to this man?" the pastor asked.

Uncle Jack grinned. "I do." He kissed her cheek.

"Thank you, Uncle Jack. I love you." Sadie kissed him back. He passed her hand over to Robbie and he took it and smiled into her eyes. Aunt Beth pushed the wheelchair up behind Jack and he collapsed back into it. The effort had sapped his strength.

Robbie heard no words. He couldn't drag his eyes from his bride's beaming face. He must've given the right responses at the right time because his brain registered the words. "Robbie, you may kiss your bride."

He grinned and put his hands on her waist. She ignored the pain and put her arms around his neck. He looked her in the eye and whispered. "I love you."

Sadie smiled at him, and he leaned in and kissed her deeply to the cheers and hollers of the congregation. Tim clapped loudly and whistled; he slapped Robbie on the back.

Finally, they broke the kiss, and the applause increased. The pastor lifted his hands to silence them. "Ladies and gentlemen, Mr. and Mrs. Robert Gordon."

Robbie closed his eyes and took a deep, contented breath. He'd gained a family, and his identity, everything he ever wanted. He still couldn't quite believe it. A wave of overwhelming joy washed through him, and he scooped his bride into his arms and spun her around. She thrust her arms around his neck and grinned. "Put me down." She chuckled, and he laughed wildly, remembering the first time he'd carried her.

Robbie kissed her again and walked out of the church with her in his arms. Sadie laid her head on his shoulder and he kissed her hair. He turned at the door. "Come on you lot, let's have lunch at the café."

The congregation laughed and turned to follow them.

Sixteen

Sadie felt eyes on her before she even opened hers. She smiled and opened them and looked up into the eyes of her beloved, with his head propped up on his hand, watching her. A wide grin crossed his face.

"What's got you smiling like that, Mr. Gordon?"

He bent down to kiss her. "You, Mrs. Gordon."

She put her hand on his cheek. "I love you, Robbie. I'm so glad you decided to stay."

Robbie exhaled deeply. "You have no idea how glad I am that Miss Neville came up with the idea of us getting married to save your reputation."

"We ought to send her a thank you card." Sadie grinned at him.

Robbie laughed and kissed her deeply. Her cheeks flushed and she closed her eyes. Robbie winked at her. "Of course, your reputation is utterly ruined now. You can never go back."

Sadie grinned at him. "I don't ever want to go back, and I'm glad my reputation is ruined because it means I'm your wife."

He became serious then. "Are you happy?"

"What kind of question is that?"

"We've been married a week. Are you happy?"

"I never knew what happy was until now, Robbie. You're everything I want in a husband. I told you that you would be."

He fell back against the pillow. "Thank you. I never thought I was anything much. You make me the man I am."

"Oh, Robbie. You're already that man."

"Well, Dear Wife, we ought to get up. Aunt Beth is coming for a visit today."

"I can't wait, I miss her in a way, but I'll miss Uncle Jack even more."

He stood and came around the bed, helped her up, and held her close. He whispered against her hair. "I'm sorry. I know how much you love him."

"Yes. But I love you more."

Robbie looked her in the eye. "It thrills me to hear you say that. I really never thought I'd ever hear that. Thanks for making me settle down."

She leaned back to look at him. "So now that you've been a husband for a week, is it as hard as you thought it would be?"

He grinned. "Not when you have the most amazing wife." They shared another long kiss and stood holding each other for a time. Eventually, they stepped back to prepare for the day.

"I'm sorry you have to help me dress and do my hair." She grimaced as she sat before the mirror and he picked up her brush.

He grinned at her in the mirror and bent down to kiss her cheek. "Don't be. I enjoy it. Thank you for allowing me to help you. It thrills me to do so." He watched her for a time as he pulled the brush through her dark hair.

"Thank you for wanting to. Sorry I gave you such a hard time the first times we met."

"Hey, you got my attention."

She rolled her eyes. "You want another reading lesson today?"

"Yes, Ma'am, if you can fit me in." He stroked the brush through her hair. "You're so beautiful, your hair is beautiful, and you smell amazing."

"Thank you, Robbie. You're not so bad yourself, you know."

"Thank you. And thank you for taking the time to teach me to read and write. I'm grateful to you."

"It's my pleasure. You're doing so well, picking it up so quickly."

Robbie shrugged. "I thought I was too stupid to learn to read and write."

Sadie scowled at him. "Robbie Gordon, how dare you call the man I love, stupid. He's the best man I know and very intelligent."

"Yes, Ma'am. I apologize."

She softened and smiled at him. "So, you should. You never were stupid, Robbie. You just missed out on learning that. But you're learning now, and I'm proud of you."

He bent down and kissed her cheek. "Thank you. Your faith in me makes me stronger."

"I love you, Robbie Gordon."

"I love you too." He placed the brush down and helped her up. "Come on, let's have breakfast at the café. It's time we entered the wide world as a married couple."

"I'd like that. It's not fair that you've had to help with all the cooking." She grimaced. "Thanks to this useless hand." She dropped her head.

Robbie lifted her chin and looked her in the eye. "Stop worrying about that. I love helping you and working alongside you. Do you know how wonderful it is to have someone depend on me and to depend on? After a lifetime of loneliness, my heart has found a home at last. Darling, I'm overjoyed to do these things for you. And with all you do in return, I can never compete."

"It's not a competition, Husband. I love you, you know. And I'm awful proud of you."

"I'm proud of you too."

*　*　*　*

Robbie stood by the graveside with an arm around his wife and aunt. Both women sobbed, and he shed a few tears of his own. He'd come to love Uncle Jack, and he'd been so encouraging as Robbie came to terms with running the livery. He was loving the job, and Sadie helped as she was able. Now that her wrist had healed, he was having a hard time trying to get her to take it easy.

The last of the dirt was patted down over the grave, and Beth stepped forward. "Goodbye, my love." She placed a flower onto the dirt. "I had a wonderful life."

Robbie wrapped both arms around Sadie, and she laid her cheek against his chest. Watching her cry made his heart ache. He realized Tim had been right,

161

and he couldn't believe he'd been worried about learning to be a husband and having a family. It was the most natural thing in the world to love Sadie and Aunt Beth. Now that Uncle Jack was gone, he felt twice as protective. He was the man of the family now. He trembled a little. *God give me the strength and wisdom to lead these women. Make me worthy of them and of You.*

Sadie sniffed loudly and he kissed her hair and passed her his handkerchief. "Are you okay?"

"I will be, with your arms around me."

"They always will be."

"Thank you." She took his hand and walked forward to the grave and stood next to Aunt Beth. "Goodbye, Uncle Jack."

Robbie slipped an arm around both woman's waists and kissed both heads.

Beth took a deep breath. "Let's go home."

"I'm sorry, Aunt Beth." Robbie squeezed her.

She nodded. "He's with Jesus. I wouldn't wish him back from Glory just because I'm sad."

"You'll join him one day, Aunty." Sadie gave her a sad smile.

"In the meantime, let's live to make him proud." Beth squared her shoulders resolutely.

"Absolutely." Robbie offered his aunt his left arm and his wife his right. He sighed and led them home, trembling somewhat at the overwhelming responsibility ahead of him.

Seventeen

Sadie perused the telegram. "Oh."

"What is it?"

She looked up at her husband and read the brief message.

'Injured. Unable to deliver horses to you. H. T. Warren.'

"What will you do?"

Robbie shrugged. "Go get them myself, I suppose."

"But the other fifteen horses will arrive from the Martins as well and you promised Mr. Taylor you'd get them to the ranch tomorrow afternoon."

Robbie scratched his chin. "I still can. I'll leave before first light. I can make it to the Warren farm by midday, then be home around five if I push them hard enough."

"Martin is arriving at four with the other fifteen horses? Do you want me to take them out to the ranch?"

"No, Sadie. Put them in the large corral at the livery and when I get home, I'll drive them out to the ranch."

"I can do it."

"You can't drive fifteen horses out there on your own?"

"Yes, I can." Sadie squinted her eyes. She didn't like to be told she 'can't' do anything, not even by the man she loved.

Robbie smiled and tenderly tucked a loose curl behind her ear. "Sadie, my love. You don't have any experience driving a large number of horses. It's too dangerous for you to do so. Besides, there is any number of hazards out at the ranch, that you aren't familiar with."

Sadie stepped back from him. Robbie could see the fire in her eyes. He'd seen that look before. She squinted at him and thrust her hands on her hips. "I may not've done it before, but I'm capable in the saddle. Just as good as you, and you've never driven that many horses before either."

"No, not that many..."

She cut him off. "So, what's the difference?"

Robbie raised his brows. "I don't want you to do it. I'll do it when I come home."

"But the horses will arrive late. At least I can get fifteen to him on time."

Robbie's face became uncharacteristically stern, but his words remained gentle. "Sadie, you're not to take those horses on your own."

"But, I can manage. It'll save you..."

Robbie raised his brows again. "No, Sadie. I forbid it." The words were out before he thought about how they came across.

Her eyes widened, and Robbie could see her face redden and the anger brewing in her eyes. "You forbid it?"

Robbie exhaled and kept his voice very calm. "Yes. I'm the man in this family, and I'm asking you not to do this."

"Why?"

"I told you why, Sadie. You're inexperienced, and it could be very dangerous."

"Because I'm a woman?"

He nodded.

She thrust her hands on her hips. "So, I'm just a weak little woman to you. Too pathetic to do a job like that."

Robbie closed his eyes and touched both her shoulders. "Darling, that is not at all what I meant. You didn't let me finish."

She brushed his hands away. "I didn't need you to finish. I understand. I'm just a weak little woman who needs a big strong man to help me."

"Sadie..."

"Hmpfff." Sadie stamped her feet. "I'm going to bed. May I have your permission to do that, Your Highness," she spat sarcastically.

"Sadie, that's not fair."

"Not fair! I'll tell you what's not fair. Being forbidden to do something I'm quite capable of doing by the man who claims he loves me."

"I do love you. That's why I don't want you to do this."

Sadie pursed her lips tightly and growled, stamped her foot, and hurried to their bedroom.

Robbie sighed and returned their coffee cups to the kitchen. He washed and dried the dishes, put them all away, and took his time wiping the counters and the table.

He extinguished all the lamps, and headed for the bedroom. It was already dark, and Sadie was in bed.

Her face turned toward the window, her back to him. He could hear her quiet sniffs and shaky breaths, and he knew she was crying. He exhaled loudly. *Lord, please comfort her.* He quickly changed and climbed into bed next to her. There would be no devotion time that evening. She didn't turn over and snuggle into him as she usually did. She didn't give him a goodnight kiss.

Robbie pulled himself close to her and put one arm around her waist. He kissed her cheek and whispered. "Goodnight, my darling. I love you so very much."

She didn't respond. Robbie kissed her again and rolled away. Laying one hand under his head, he stared at the ceiling and spent a lot of time in prayer.

Rising early, as he said he would, Robbie changed quickly. He walked around to Sadie's side of the bed and knelt to look at her in the low light. Her face was stained with her tears. He pushed her hair back off her face. In some ways, he was glad she was asleep. He didn't want a repeat of last night's conversation.

"Goodbye my love. I'll see you this evening." He kissed her forehead. "I love you so very much."

With another glance at the beautiful woman he loved, he stood and hurried away to see to his task.

*   *   *   *

Sadie slopped the batter into the pan and groaned.

Aunt Beth looked up from setting the table. "What's gotten into you this morning? Missing your husband?"

"No." Sadie scowled. "I don't want to talk to him today anyway."

"Why ever not?" Aunt Beth walked to the kitchen and put the coffee pot on.

"The nerve of that man. How dare he treat me like that." Sadie seethed.

Aunt Beth's head snapped up and she hurried over to Sadie. "Did he hurt you?" She couldn't even fathom the thought.

Sadie closed her eyes and sighed. "No, Aunt Beth, Robbie would never hurt me. I know that much. Least not physically."

Beth nodded and gave her a knowing smile. "So, he hurt your feelings then?"

Sadie scowled at the older woman. "He had the nerve to actually forbid me from taking the horses to the ranch."

Beth looked at her like she was waiting for the audacious part.

"He forbade me, Aunt Beth. He actually said the words, 'I forbid you.'"

"And?"

"And?" Sadie said incredulously, thrusting her hands in the air and flicking pancake batter across the floor.

"Well, why did he forbid you?"

"He said I wasn't experienced at driving a large number of horses, and it was too dangerous for a woman."

"Sounds reasonable to me."

"Reasonable?" Sadie flipped a pancake with vengeance.

"Yes, it sounds to me, like he's trying to protect you."

"I don't need his protection. I'm quite capable."

"Sadie, you're being unreasonable."

Sadie glared at her aunt. "What if Uncle Jack had forbidden you to do something?"

"He did on a number of occasions."

Sadie furrowed her brows. "What did you do?"

Beth smiled. "I honored his request."

"You did?"

"Of course, I did, Sadie. Robbie is your husband. He loves you, and he cares about you. He's the leader of your family, and you need to honor his wishes. He wouldn't have said that if he didn't have good reason to. He isn't wrong. You aren't experienced, and it could be dangerous. You aren't familiar with the ranch, and you could get hurt."

"Well, I don't care. I'm going to show him he's wrong. I'm not a pathetic little weak woman."

"That would be a waste of time."

"Why, because he's too stubborn to listen?"

"No, because he already knows you aren't weak."

Sadie groaned and turned her attention back to their breakfast.

*   *   *   *

Sadie stood, fetched her coat, and opened the door.

Aunt Beth looked up from her knitting. "Are you going to meet Mr. Martin?"

"Yes. He's supposed to be here with the fifteen horses at four."

"And what are you going to do?"

"I told you, Aunt Beth. I'm going to take them out to the ranch."

"What about Robbie's words."

"Oh, he was just being a man. I'm quite capable."

"Sadie, Dear, I think you should listen to him."

"I plan to show him I'm quite capable." She stormed out the door.

"Oh, no. She's so strong-willed." Beth put down her knitting. "Lord, watch over her, please."

Eighteen

"Thank you, Mr. Martin." Sadie paid the man and shut the corral gate on the fifteen horses. The man nodded and jumped on his horse, his companion was already mounted and waiting. They both tipped their hat to Sadie and galloped away.

Sadie turned to look at the horses. "If he can drive them, so can I," she determined. Each horse had a simple rope halter, to make it easier to lead. She ran into the livery and found two long lengths of rope. She tied one end to the first horse's halter, then wove it through each halter until the horses were linked together the same way Mr. Martin had.

She saddled Smokey and tied a long rope to the last horse and to her saddle.

"Success." She spoke to the air as she slowly headed towards the ranch, with the horses following along behind. "See, this isn't so hard. I don't know what Robbie's problem was."

*　*　*　*

"Thank you, Warren. These are fine horses. My client will be happy."

"Very good, Mr. Gordon. You care for a bite before you go home?"

"No, thank you, Sir. I just want to get back to my wife."

The shine in his eye made Warren chuckle. "Newlyweds?"

Robbie grinned. "Been married a little over a month."

"Well, no wonder you don't want to eat with an old bachelor like me. Get going with you."

Robbie nodded, leaped up on his horse, and gripped the rope attached to the horses behind him. He tied it to the horn of his saddle and walked out of town. He sighed as he headed for home. "Lord, I pray she'll forgive me for my insistence. I love her strength and stubbornness, but I hope she can understand I'm just trying to protect her. She's the most precious person in the world to me, and the thought of her being hurt again..." he closed his eyes and sighed. "I couldn't bear it, Lord."

*   *   *   *

Weary and somewhat hungry, Robbie rode into Dusty Ridge around the time he expected to. Approaching the house, he looked across at the livery. No horses stood in the corral. "Hmmm, maybe Martin is running late."

As he pulled up at the corral and halted the horses, Aunt Beth came running out of the house. "Robbie." Her expression caused Robbie's heart to leap to his throat.

"What is it, Aunt Beth?"

"It's Sadie. She drove the horses out to the ranch."

"What?" Robbie's face curled up in pain. "I told her not to."

Beth wiped away a tear. "She was so determined to show you she wasn't weak. I tried to talk her out of it."

Robbie rolled his eyes and gulped. "Oh no. I'll find her, Aunt Beth. I promise."

She nodded. "I'll get supper on."

"Great, I'll be back in a couple of hours or so." Robbie nodded to her, clucked to his horse, and headed for the ranch, he nudged Comet into a canter, and the roped horses followed.

*   *   *   *

Sadie rode into the ranch. "I don't know what his problem is. I can do this." She grinned. Uncertain of the exact location for the horses, she turned up a path between some scraggly bushes. She could see one of the herds ahead of her and knew the cowboys would be there. She'd ask one of them.

Just as she reached the herd, a hawk flew across her path and caused skittish Smokey to rear, it frightened the following horses, and they bolted, roped together they took off toward the herd; Smokey was drawn along between the other horses, trying to keep up.

Robbie hurried into the ranch and headed for the corrals. Turner was waiting for him.

"Rob. These are fine..." Turner's voice was cut off by a scream.

Robbie gasped. "Sadie," he yelled, thrust the rope holding the horses to Turner, and bolted in the direction of the scream.

He approached the stampeding horses. Sadie was holding on for dear life, but it was clear Smokey was struggling to keep up with the much larger horses. "Sadie," Robbie yelled.

"Hellllp!" Sadie had no choice but to be dragged along with them.

Lloyd and Flynn galloped towards them and tried to surround the horses, but they kept running. Robbie galloped alongside. "Sadie, hold on."

Sadie's terrified eyes turned to his. "Helpppp."

Robbie grabbed at the ropes to try to halt the horses. He pulled Comet in amongst the horses, keeping pace with them. He forced his way through the horses to Sadie. Comet kept pace with the other horses, stumbling and desperately trying to keep up. He reached Sadie and yanked her off Smokey, hoisting her into the saddle in front of him.

"Pass her to me," Flynn called. There was one horse between he and Robbie.

"Put your hands out. Flynn will get you to safety." He spoke gently to her, terrified she would fall and be crushed by the horses. Holding her tightly, Robbie leaned as far as he could across the horse next to him. Flynn managed to reach her waist and lifted her onto his horse, then immediately halted his own and helped her to the ground.

Relieved Sadie was safe, Robbie tried to pull in the horses, but they darted to the side to avoid a bush, and Smokey tripped and knocked into Comet, causing Robbie to fall from his horse. He fell between the bolting horses, and the four following horses rode right over him.

"Robbie," Sadie screamed. Her hands flew to her face.

Lloyd hurried over and checked for a pulse. "He's alive..."

Flynn rode up.

"But he's weak. Gotta get him to the doc." Lloyd stood.

"I'll get Edwards. He can get Turner and the others, they'll go after the horses, and you get Robbie to the Doc." Flynn galloped off.

Lloyd nodded. Sadie was leaning over Robbie holding his hand and weeping. "I'm so sorry, Robbie, I'm so sorry." Robbie groaned, and Sadie began to weep.

Lloyd put a hand on her shoulder. "He'll be okay, Mrs. Gordon. He's strong."

"What's wrong with him?"

"Can't rightly say, I ain't a doctor, but we'll get him to the doc." He smiled and gripped her arm.

She nodded and stroked Robbie's brow. "I'm sorry, my darling, I'm so sorry." She wept heavily.

Edwards rode up with the wagon and Jerry on horseback. "Help me get him on." Edwards gestured to the two cowboys. "Then, Jerry, go and help round up those horses."

The two men nodded, and they carefully lifted Robbie onto the back of the wagon.

Edwards put his hand out to Sadie and helped her up on the wagon. "He'll be alright, Mrs. Gordon."

She smiled and sat down next to him, clinging to his hand.

"I'll get him to the doc." He nodded to the young cowboys. "Jerry, you go after Flynn and those horses."

"I'll stay with the herd," Lloyd offered.

Edwards nodded and leaped up on the wagon hurrying toward town.

*   *   *   *

Sadie sat beside the bed in the clinic and wept. She clung to Robbie's hand and prayed without ceasing. Aunt Beth put her arm around her niece and continued the prayers.

"How could I have been so foolish?"

"What are you saying?" Aunt Beth asked.

"This is all my fault."

"How so?"

"If I had just listened to him...."

Beth squeezed Sadie. "Don't, Sadie, don't beat yourself up. The doctor said Robbie's going to be fine. He's just battered and bruised. Learn from this, Darling."

"I didn't even tell him I loved him before he left. I was trying to punish him."

"He knows you love him."

Sadie nodded. "Why am I so stubborn?"

Beth smiled. "All I know for sure is Robbie loves you fiercely, Sadie."

"It's the second time he's saved my life." She trembled and closed her eyes. "I don't deserve him."

175

"Sadie." Robbie's voice was croaky and weak.

Sadie snapped her head around and gripped Robbie's hand. "Oh, you're awake. Praise God." Her tears overflowed again. Beth hurried away to get the doctor.

"How are you feeling, Mr. Gordon?" The doctor put his hand to Robbie's arm.

"A little worse for wear." Robbie chuckled. He flashed a smile at Sadie, whose face was curled up in agony.

"Fortunately, you have no major injuries." The doctor stepped back.

"Can we take him home, Doc?" Sadie asked.

"Yeah, he just needs to take it easy for a few days, but I'm confident he has no major injuries." The doctor nodded and turned to Robbie. "You're a lucky man, it could've been so much worse."

"Thanks, Doc." Robbie nodded.

Sadie and the doctor helped him up, and he hobbled home clinging to Sadie. At last, she had him seated before the fire in the armchair. Aunt Beth had excused herself; it had been a long night.

Sadie hovered around, trying to busy herself with something. Robbie gripped her hand as she walked past.

She looked at him and her lips trembled.

He gestured for her to sit on his lap.

"But, I don't want to hurt you."

"I don't care. Please, I want to hold you."

She nodded and climbed up on his knee. He winced as she hit one of his bruised legs.

"Sorry." She grimaced.

He winked. "Totally worth it." Sadie lay back against his arm.

Robbie put his hand on her cheek and his eyes filled with tears. "I'm so glad you weren't hurt."

Sadie closed her eyes, her lips trembled, and she burst into tears. He wrapped her in his arms and held her while she shook. He rubbed her back and lay his head against hers.

"I'm so sorry." She wept. "Robbie, oh, I'm sorry."

He squeezed her. "Shhhh, Sadie, my darling. I'm just so glad you're safe and well."

She sat back to look at him. He smiled kindly at her and brushed away a tear with his thumb. He kissed her hair.

"You aren't angry?"

Robbie smiled and stroked her cheek. "No, I'm not angry. I'm just relieved. When I saw you amongst those stampeding horses, I was so scared. I couldn't bear to lose you, Sadie. You're the most important person in the world to me." He closed his eyes and shuddered. "I never imagined I could have a family and now that I have you, I don't plan to lose you." He winked.

Sadie nodded. "I understand. I felt the same way when I saw you fall off the horse. I'm so sorry. I should've listened to you. I'm so stubborn."

"No. Sadie, don't. I love your stubbornness, and I don't want you to be anyone you're not."

"But I defied you. You were right, and I defied you."

He squeezed her and leaned his head against hers. "I'm so sorry that you felt hurt when I asked you not to go to the ranch..."

She cut him off. "No. It's fine, you were right, and I'm just a silly girl who doesn't want to listen."

Robbie's lips trembled and a tear ran down his cheek.

Sadie wiped it away and raised her brows in question.

"Oh, Sadie. You're my precious wife. You're not a silly girl, you're a tenacious and strong woman, and I love that. I need your strength and your stubbornness. If you weren't that way, I would've left town and missed out on this life."

"I just got so mad when you forbade me."

Robbie smiled. "I'm sorry that I did."

She shrugged. "Turns out you were right. I should've trusted you as the husband, leader, and head of our family."

"I may be the head of our family, Sadie, but you're the neck. Just think how useless a head would be without a neck to turn it."

"You're kind, but I know as a Christian woman, I should obey my husband. I'm sorry. Will you forgive me?"

He smiled, stroked her cheek and leaned in and kissed her deeply.

"I'll take that as a yes." Her cheeks warmed.

"Of course, I forgive you, Sadie. I've never loved anyone like I love you. I love you so much that it makes my bones ache. The thought of being without you terrifies me. You're precious to me, and I didn't want to see you get hurt."

She nodded, and tears pooled in the corners of her eyes.

"It is my God-given role to be the leader of our family, and honestly, it's a terrifying responsibility. I feel so unworthy and so inadequate for the task, but with God's help, I'll do my best to honor and lead you in the way you deserve to be led. Oh, Sadie, I promise I'll never just lord my manliness over you. When I draw a line, it's because I want you to be safe."

She nodded. "You're a wonderful leader and man. I love you so much, Robbie. I'm sorry I'm so strong-willed. I promised when we got married that I'd obey you, and here we've been married a little over a month, and I'm defying you already."

"Mrs. Gordon, you're human. So am I. We're going to fail each other; we're going to get things wrong sometimes. But I will always love you, always protect you, always serve you, no matter what. And we can get through these things together."

"I don't deserve you, Robbie." She lay her head on his shoulder.

Robbie closed his eyes and sighed. He kissed her hair. "Don't say that. You do deserve me. I don't want you to change who you are, Sadie. I didn't marry a demure little weaking. I married this feisty beauty, and I couldn't be more thrilled. I hope we have a daughter just like you someday."

She grinned and put her arms around his neck. They sat in silence for a time. Sadie sighed. "Thank you for saving my life again."

Robbie lifted her chin and kissed her. "You don't have to thank me. I'll move heaven and earth to save you."

"I'm sorry you got hurt saving me." Sadie brushed at a bruise on his forehead.

"It's okay, Darling. I'd much rather it was me that was hurt. I'd lay down my life for you. I told you that in the cabin. I meant it then and I mean it now."

Sadie had no words, so she kissed him, prolonging it as long as she could.

"Phew." Robbie grinned. "That was some kiss, Mrs. Gordon. Makes my head spin."

She smiled. "We ought to turn in."

"You're right."

Sadie gestured to climb off his knee, but he gripped her tightly and stood up with her in his arms. She giggled and let him carry her to their bedroom. He put her back on her feet and slipped his arms around her waist, pulling her against him. "I'm in love with you, Mrs. Gordon."

She kissed him again. "I'm in love with you, Mr. Gordon."

"There are no sweeter words, Wife."

They prepared for bed and sat up together, spending time praying and petitioning God to help them both honor and love each other the way He planned them to.

As she snuggled into her husband's arms, she laid her head on his chest. "Thanks for loving me so much that you're willing to take a stand. You're a wonderful leader for our family. I'm so proud of you, and I trust you to lead."

Robbie kissed her hair and sniffed away a tear. "Thank you," was all he could manage. He squeezed her tightly, thankful the day hadn't ended in tragedy.

Epilogue

"This is my favorite verse. Have a go." Sadie passed the Bible to Robbie and pointed to the verse.

Robbie nodded and focused on the words. "F- for God so l... lo – ved. Loved." He looked at Sadie. Her wide smile encouraged him to continue. "...the w... wor led?"

"World."

He nodded and went back to the beginning. "For God so loved the world." He pointed at each word as he read them. "th...at that he gave his on-ly begger?" He looked to her.

"Be-gott-en."

"Begotten. Gave his only begotten Son. That who..."

"Who-so-ever."

"Whosoever be-live eth. Believeth."

She nodded. "Keep going, my love. You're doing wonderfully." She kissed his cheek.

"That helps." He grinned.

"Keep going."

"That who-so-ever believeth in him sh sh old...

"Should."

He frowned.

"Silent l."

He grimaced. "All these silent letters. It's so confusing."

"You're doing great."

He nodded. "Should not per sh."

"Perish."

"Perish but have ev-er-last-ing, everlasting leaf."

"Look again."

Robbie concentrated. "Oh, it has an e on the end. So, the i says its own name," he recalled. "So, it would be life?" He looked to her for confirmation.

Sadie grinned and gripped his arm. "Well done. Oh. I'm so proud of you. You've picked this up so quickly. I knew you would."

"Your faith in me has made all the difference. I wish I could pick up writing as quickly." He screwed up his face.

"Hey, it's only been a little over three months. You're doing better than you think." She smiled kindly.

"I couldn't do it without you."

"I'm happy to help you."

"I'd like to write a letter to Timothy and one to Mrs. Bonnie. They'll both be amazed to see me writing in my own hand."

"I'll help you, if you like."

"Thank you."

"Have another go at the verse." She squeezed his arm.

He nodded. "For God so loved the word... world that he gave his only be-gott-en Son, that who-so-ev-er believeth in him should?"

She nodded.

"Should not perish, but have ever-lasting life."

Sadie clapped and tears filled her eyes.

"What?"

"I'm just so proud of you."

"For being able to do something children can do?" He grimaced.

"Stop that, Robbie Gordon. You just missed out on the learning. I'm proud of you."

"Thank you, Darling."

"Shall we write a letter?"

"I'd like that. I can't wait for Timothy to see I've written and Mrs. Bonnie too. She'll be thrilled."

"She'll be as proud of you as I am."

"I'd like to send her a photograph of our wedding day."

"Great idea. I'll get the paper and a pen."

Sadie had a sly grin on her face as she sat back down.

"What?" Robbie squinted at her. "You look like the mouse that got the cheese."

"I have something for you."

"You do?"

"Mmmhmmm." She passed him an envelope; it had his name on the front.

"What is this?"

"You'll have to read it to find out."

"What's going on?"

"Read it."

He nodded and opened the envelope and slipped out a small card.

"Read it out loud."

He squinted at her. The look on her face made him curious.

"Go on." She was as excited as a child at Christmas.

"Okay." He looked at the words.

He read loudly. "I can-t... oh can't. I can't wait to meet you in Ju-ly?"

She nodded and grinned.

Robbie screwed up his brows and looked at her. "What does this mean? Who's meeting me in July?"

Sadie glanced at the paper and grinned at him.

Robbie kept reading. "Love Ba-by Gordon." He gasped and looked at her. "Baby Gordon?"

She bit her lip and nodded, placing a hand on her abdomen.

"You're having a baby?" His face lit up.

"Mmmhmm." She grinned.

Robbie stood up and hauled Sadie into his arms. He spun her around and put her down. "Oh, I can't believe it."

"Doctor Chapman told me today, I'm about two months along. I was so excited to have you read it for yourself. Our child is going to be so proud of his daddy."

"It's a boy?"

She shrugged. "I don't know, could be."

"I kinda hope it's a girl." He chuckled.

"Are you happy?"

Robbie's eyes became very intense, and he pulled Sadie close and kissed her deeply.

"I'll take that as a yes." She grinned.

"I'm beyond happy, Wife. I can't wait. I can't believe I was ever afraid to have a family. Now I'm beyond thrilled, excited, over the moon. You've made me the happiest man in the world, Mrs. Gordon. You've single-handedly redeemed me and given me a life beyond my wildest dreams."

"I think we've redeemed each other."

"You're right." He winked at her.

"So, no more roaming for you?"

"Never again. I'm settled, home. At long last I belong to someone and something."

"Praise the Lord."

"Praise the Lord, indeed. I love you so much, Mrs. Gordon."

"I love you too, Robbie."

He pulled her into a warm embrace and leaned his head down to kiss her. At last, laying his forehead on hers, he sighed contentedly. "Thank you. I kinda wish I didn't have to go to work today. I'd rather just stand here and hold you all day."

"We have to work, Husband."

He leaned back to look her in the eye. "No more for you. I don't want you to catch something from the livery."

"I'll be okay," she argued, but her conscience pricked her as memory of the horse-stampede entered her mind.

"Don't argue, Wife. Don't make me get Aunt Beth onto you." He chuckled as the older woman entered the room.

Beth looked from shining face to shining face. "What's going on?"

Sadie tucked her lips under and looked at her feet. Her face flushed. Robbie kissed Sadie's cheek and grinned at Beth.

Beth frowned and squinted at them. Sadie looked up and gave her a shy smile. Something clicked. "Ohhhh." Beth put both hands to her face and gushed, "A baby?"

Sadie nodded.

"Oh, Sadie, Darling." Beth ran to embrace her. "I'm so happy for you."

She released Sadie and wrapped her arms around Robbie. "I'm so proud of you and delighted for you. Ben would be ecstatic to know he has a grandchild on the way."

"Thanks, Aunt Beth. I'm thrilled. All these years of not knowing who I am and not having a family, and now I have more than I could ever dream of." He wrapped his arms around his wife and kissed her deeply.

The End

If you enjoyed this book and want to read more in this series then check out the series page on amazon for more great titles.

https://www.amazon.com/dp/BoBNKN43TP

About the Author

Jo Dawson grew up on a dairy farm in Wellsford, a small town in the North Island of New Zealand. She spent fifteen years as a teacher in New Zealand and abroad before becoming a stay-at-home mum and completing her graduate degree in Theology.

She has lived in Australia and the USA for a time, and these experiences have added to her love of people and history. Blessed with a vivid imagination and a love of classical literature and historical fiction, Jo virtually grew up best friends with Anne Shirley, romping with Jo March and her sisters, sailing a raft down the Mississippi with Huckleberry Finn or living in the 'little house' with Laura Ingalls.

Born and raised in a strong Christian family, Jo's faith is at the centre of who she is, with a lifetime of being involved in churches and Christian camps. These two loves; literature and the Lord, have inevitably converged into writing compelling stories of strong Christian women courageously facing the hardships of life on the frontier. It is her hope that women of all ages would find encouragement from her heroines' experiences that, while fiction, so often mirror even our modern lives.

Jo currently resides in the small North Island town of Waipu in New Zealand, where she lives with her husband, son, father-in-law and a very lazy cat.